I0452042

Once Loved Innocence Lost

Part 2

Help Me Lord

Written by

Natasha Garry

P.O. Box 402
Swiftwater, PA 18370
(973) 348-5067
sspublishingcompany@gmail.com
www.sharsheypublishingcompany.com

Copyright © 2020 Natasha Garry
ISBN:13- 978-1-7348030-2-0
Publisher: Shar- Shey Publishing Company LLC
Book Cover Designed by: Dynasty's Visionary Designs
Edited by: ATW Editing

DEDICATION:

First, I thank my Heavenly Father, for making ways out of no ways. To my beautiful children: Chanel, Talid, Keiffon, Ameillya, and Tiffany. Mommy loves you guys so much. To my love: my husband for his support. To my sisters and brother. To my publisher for giving me a chance, and to the editor: thank you guys so much.

ONCE LOVED INNOCENCE LOST: PART 2
HELP ME LORD

B eing married, I thought it would and could be a happier ever after. Well, that's what television led me to believe, once when I was a child. Once I became an adult and got married, marriage was no cake and ice cream. Nor was it any sweet smell of roses. I've been married two times. Boy, did I experience more bitter than sweet.

My first marriage was oil and vinegar; we did not mix. No matter how much sex I gave my husband, no matter how I tried to make my marriage work, he always made it into another woman's bed. He could not keep his dick in his pants. He was very controlling and sometimes abusive. I tried to be submissive and make my marriage work. But after many women contacting me, and him leaving me on numerous occasions, that submissive shit went out the door. I got over being submissive real quick. My only reason for taking him back was I did not want to be a single parent again, especially now for the third time, and I did not want to raise my children without a father figure.

I also took my ex-husband back because of my need for sex. I just had to have it, every day if I could. I did not want to be a sinner sleeping with so many men, as I'd done in the past. Some of the men I slept with was for my personal pleasure, and the other sixty percent was so I could support my five children.

My ex-husband did not help me take care of the last three children I had with him. His way of supporting them was letting Child Support take out $120.00 from his paycheck every week. No extra—he wouldn't even take them to the doctors, and he didn't even show up to the school plays or teacher conferences. Of my other two children's fathers, one just paid $78.00 through Child Support, but would argue with me every time he had to go and pay. He liked to call me all kinds of insults, and he wanted me to drop the child support. I agreed to drop the child support one day. Once I dropped the child support, he still didn't do anything to help. So three months later, I had to add the child support back on him. He was back at verbally abusing me once again. He didn't care who heard him disrespecting me. With the other baby daddy, I only received two child support checks from him of $38.00. After that, he quit his job. He was not actively involved in his child's life. Three years later, I heard from my cousin that he got deported. I never found out why he got deported.

I never knew why I could never keep a man, let alone my baby daddies. As soon as I said I was pregnant, they were gone. Oh, well. Who cares? I still had to take care of my children. I can't worry about their dads leaving me. I didn't plan on having so many baby daddies. Three was too much for me. I dreamed when I was younger I'd have one man/husband and have seven children. Life didn't turn out that way. Through my many bad experiences with men, I learned to get over them real quick.

This one man taught me a learning lesson at age 15. He was 25 years old. Back then, I did not like to have sex much. I didn't know what I was supposed to enjoy out of sex; all I knew was that sex was painful and he was abusive. He was at times gentle and soft-spoken. But his famous line he said to me was: "I could walk into a group of girls and walk out with one of them, and get over you real quick." That line stuck with me and I used that line with some added words to it. If a man threatened to dump me, I would say to them, "The same way I met you is the same way I could meet another man; there are too many men out there for me to cry over one." Some men didn't like me saying stuff like that to them. They'd be wanting me to be emotional and beg them to stay. In the past, I might have, but with the growing pains, I'd be like "see ya."

I learned real quick never to shed any tears in front of a man breaking up with me. Especially when they are really disrespectful with their break-ups with me. Some of the stuff these men can say can be horrible. I guess it made them feel good to try and hurt my feelings and try to put me down. Don't worry, my mouth was just as reckless. If I cared for him, I waited until I was by myself, and got one good cry in my room for a while and got over him. I listened to my break-up songs while crying. But through my past experiences, I learned not to have feelings anymore. I learned not to trust men anymore.

If a man was being nice to me, sometimes I got to wondering, "Why is he being nice? What is he looking for, or what do he want?" Because in my past experiences, men don't do anything for nothing. Relationships I experienced were an exchange. When I say exchange, I mean if a man is spending his time with you, later on, he is going to want some ass. If he buys you something, he's gonna want some ass. If he does anything plain and simple and you don't have a job, you're a single mother, and you need him to help you with something, best to believe he wants some of your ass. Now, I'm not saying all men are like this. This is based on my experience.

Maybe I could have said no and made these men wait, but one, I was hot in the pants, and two, I needed their cash to help me buy pampers, food, and bus fares to get my kids to the doctor. Just to remind you, I was a single parent. It was very hard to get a good job with five little ones. The other reason I learned not to say no to sex is some men can't handle the word no, and they lie and say you got them all excited. Even if you've done nothing but sit there and have a normal conversation with them, trying your hardest not to let the conversation go in the direction of sex, keeping your distance away from them, sitting on another couch.

I'll tell you one of my experiences: It was just me and him alone, kids in the bed asleep, television on, and he on one couch, me on another. We were both fully clothed, but for some reason, this man starts talking about sex. I tried not to take it there with him, because I kind of liked him. I wanted to see him again. I tried to do that old school rule, make him wait. But this man didn't want to wait, he wanted the ass now. As soon as I said "no, it's late, it's time to go," now he wanted to get aggressive with me. If I knew that's what he wanted, I would not have called him over. Or I would have at least waited until I needed his help. Anyway, after that piece of shit got what he wanted, he zipped his pants and left.

Also, being molested, I guess it had a different effect on me. While some may not like sex, I grew into liking sex. Sex was a feeling for me. If I got good sex, I caught feelings; the best sex, I could say I love you to a man with no problem. I'd be ready to get married the next month, so I wouldn't continue living in sin. Horrible sex, I am not calling your ass anymore, unless I am really desperate and want a piece of wood between my legs. I guess I was a fast ass, or as some may say, a whore. I didn't plan for my life to be this way. Shame on them to judge me. Do you think I meant for this shit to happen? Do you think I wanted my life to be like this? I am struggling with an addiction, which is sex. Oh well, I can't cry over spilled milk. I am who I am. Am I proud? No, it was like a drug. I have to have it. Sex made me feel good. It was like a pleasurable comfort. Yes, I'm weird, but it doesn't feel weird; it became my new normal. My way of thinking, if my man doesn't have sex with me, he doesn't care about me. Anyway, enough of this sex talk.

Anytime I dated a new man or had a booty call, I always had one set of rules they had to follow: Don't come to my home until my children are asleep, don't talk to my children, don't look at my children, don't try to discipline my children (not even their dads could discipline my children), don't ask to spend the night, and they had to be out of my house before my children woke up. The reason for me being this way is I don't trust men. Also, I knew that if I got into a relationship, that it was only temporary, due to my past experiences. I didn't mean to be this way. But I was afraid and had no trust in men. I tried to keep my man happy. I felt bad I had to be this way towards some of these men who seemed like nice and respectable men. But the truth of the matter is, I don't trust them. Could you trust a man if you had been molested and raped plenty of times? The second reason I have trust issues with men is, when you are down on your luck, and ask him for help, he turns right around and asks for some ass, or he leaves you alone just because you asked him for help.

Now the sad thing about it is I just wanted one man in my lifetime; I did not know my future would look like this. This hurts when I have to sit here and think about it. I feel like I'm a nobody. I just wanted someone I could truly trust, truly love, truly surrender to. A man who will be there in my shortfall, and who will say "baby everything is going to be okay" even when it's not okay. Give him my all. It does hurt my heart when I have time to sit and think about it. I try to keep busy just so I don't have time to think about all this shit I had to do to survive. I didn't plan on being a single parent. I wanted my children to have a father (like what you see in those movies). I didn't plan on being alone.

I repent for all my sins; I just want to live right by God. God, you are the only man I trust. I don't want any more abusive men in my life, no more controlling men in my life. I don't want the many men running in and out of my bed and my life. God, help me please to get on my own two feet. To depend on you and not these men of the world. In Jesus' name, I pray. Amen.

*****

Speaking about controlling again, one of my relationships was so toxic, I thought about killing myself, twice. I loved him so much. I made myself believe everything he said, even though I knew he was lying. I was crying all the time. I didn't know my worth. I still don't know my worth from time to time. I used to cook his dinner, wash his clothes, clean his house, babysit his child, and did his list of chores he made for me daily. And when it came to sex, if I said no he just took it. Even if my ass was funky from being out all day, he didn't care. Our relationship ended because he kept cheating on me, hardcore. When confronted by these women, my man would lie and say that they were lying. He tried to convivence me that his cheating was all my fault for listening to these women, even though some of these women came to me with proof that they were seeing my man. My man was so manipulative and controlling. Especially when I saw him kick one woman's ass: After hearing her jaw pop from his fist, that made me really believe his threats. I didn't want him doing that to me. His hits hurt for sure, when he used to yank me up out of anger, with his fist balled up, and me covering my face. I learned to stay in my lane real quick.

Our relationship was so toxic, I had to call the crisis hotline on myself because I thought I was going crazy. I was at the point where I had thoughts of suicide. When he cheated on me, I fucked his car up and fucked his friend who came and pretended he was there for my support. When my man found out, he put a gun to my head. I said, "Pull the trigger, you already killed my heart," crying like a baby. I didn't move, nor did I try to run. I truly loved him more than myself. The sad thing was, he didn't love me back. Love is not supposed to hurt. Thank God that relationship is over. The only good thing that came from that relationship was my beautiful child. The other thing which came from that relationship was a horrible learning experience. From now on, I will guard my heart.

It took me a while to get over him. Listening to my breakup music and spending time with other men on a sexual level helped me to get over him. Enough of my flashbacks…

I need one man. I am not getting any younger. I want one or two more babies. So I need to move fast. I pray God will bless me with a man I can grow old with—someone I could trust, hold, love, and have good sex with. I'm tired of sleeping around with all these men. I need to get myself together. I really want to live right by God.

*****

I turned back around to pick up my mobile phone that I had destroyed out of anger. Damn, I am such an idiot! Like I have money to buy me a new phone. I went to the mobile store to see how much a new phone would cost me. The lady asked me for my identification and a few questions. Then she said that I was eligible for an upgrade.

"How much would an upgrade cost me?" I asked. She said it depends on what device I pick. So after looking around I picked out a phone that was better than the phone I had. I even changed my mobile phone number at the store. Thank God it didn't cost me much. I felt a lot better. New items make me happy. After she finished setting up everything, I left the store. I called my cousin to check on my children, then I told her I would be there to pick my babies up tomorrow. I was thinking about going out of town for a while. But I could not leave without my babies. She said okay, not a problem.

My ass is done with these men from my past. I don't even want to think about my situation anymore. I need to get my life together. I feel like it's just me and my children against the world. I pray that I get my life together, by the Grace of God, I pray.

I'm not going to lie. After I got off the phone, I called one of these dating lines. I started talking to men instantly. This had been going on for a while. I was 25 years old at the time. I went back on a dating phone line. I didn't know if I wanted a male or female.

I chatted with many different people. I even met a few people who wanted to see what I looked like and, of course, I wanted to see what they looked like. I met this one guy named Rocky, who was about seven years older than I was. We had a good phone conversation; we talked on the phone for quite a while. We really had a lot of common interests. I told him about my five children, and he told me about his four children. He was single and so was I.

One night, we scheduled to meet each other after I put my children to bed. He came to my townhome and met me at approximately 10:00 pm after he got off of work. He called me and said he was at the top of the hill, so I came outside to meet him. The only reason I came out to meet with him is because my neighborhood was in a rough area. Then we talked outside for about five minutes and we started to walk back to my apartment, which was townhomes connected together. He sat on my couch and pulled out his burner, which is also known as a gun. He explained that the only reason why he had it with him was that he heard about my area. What he heard was true. Shit, I was afraid sometimes to leave out with my children, but I had to act as if I wasn't. People in my area really didn't like me too much, especially my next-door neighbor with that big-ass, mean Pitbull. I used to have to yell "please get your dog," so my kids and I could get in or out of the house. She would say it doesn't bite, but I was not taking any chances.

Anyway, back to Rocky. He said, "You cute," then he asked me if he was what he described. I said, "Yes, you're attractive." So we talked for about an hour or two, and then he left. I walked him to his car and he said he would come to see me on Saturday night. I said okay, that would be cool.

For a few days, I was chatting with him and a few other men. I slept with a few of the men. Then one day, my friend who lived a block away, who I met from being a volunteer at the school my children attended, introduced me to her fiancé's best friend, Arron. He and I started talking, even talking on the phone. I just kept him as a phone buddy for now. Once in a blue, I let him come see me while four of my five children were in school. Once or twice, I went to his two-bedroom apartment, and he took me to the movies one time. But I had my daughter with me. I had no one I could trust with her, for the time being. I was unemployed and using my child support to take care of my children.

I didn't like the children's school too much, so I was there to help out and keep my eye on them almost every day. Once in a blue, I would stay home and cook and clean, or babysit one of the employees of the school's grandson. Did I want to do it? No. But I did it out of kindness, plus me and her son were friends, who I slept with maybe three times. Don't get me wrong, I loved his grandson, but it was hard walking down the street pushing two strollers. Or carrying one toddler on my hip and the other one in my arms.

So the weekend came. I was so excited that Rocky was coming over. I made sure all of my children were fed, cleaned, and in bed asleep. This time Rocky came to my home at 11:00 pm. While I was waiting for him to come over, I extra cleaned my home, washed my ass, then I waited for him to come while I was talking to my female friend on the phone. I was kind of anxious to see him. We were talking dirty on the phone. Rocky and I talked on the phone for about two months before we actually met each other. When he came over, he rang my doorbell. I was thinking to myself, "Oh, I didn't have to meet him outside this time. Okay cool, I don't have to put my shoes on." I like to walk barefoot in my home. I mop my floor every other day. I opened the door, then I sat my big ass on the couch. As soon as he closed the door, I said, "Can you please lock the door?" and he did. Then he came and sat on the couch right next to me.

We talked for about a half-hour, then he started kissing me. I'm not going to lie, but I got all excited on the inside. Then he started touching and rubbing on me and we had extremely good foreplay. I was ready. He took his pants halfway down and I just lifted my pajama gown. He put on a rubber, and he went to town. We both took turns giving each other pleasure. Right after we finished, he pulled his pants up and almost fell asleep on my couch. I said, "Oh no, you going to have to get ready to go. It's 5:00 am and I don't want my children to see you here."

He said, "Well, can I at least catch my breath?"

I said, "Yes when you get in your car."

"Okay, damn," he said, "I feel like a dirty washcloth."

I laughed and said, "I don't want my kids to see you unless you were my man, and that isn't the situation here."

He said, "Okay, I will call you tomorrow."

I was like, okay cool; I had this big Kool-Aid smile on my face. I'm not going to lie, sex was banging. It was the best sex I'd had in a while. Don't get me wrong, I'd been sleeping with other men, but it was for an even exchange. I did what they wanted and in return, they gave me money. I always supplied the condoms, because some of their asses tried to be slick and act as if they don't have a condom. It's okay; I have one.

Rocky and I were having sex for about six months now, but only on Saturday nights, because of his work schedule. I kind of trusted him because I believed he was being honest with me. One Friday he came over, and my mom happened to be over for the weekend. He met my mom by accident. I didn't plan on him coming over. He normally came on a Saturday. But this time he came on a Friday night. So since my mom was there, she normally slept on my couch and placed a blanket on the floor with pillows and sheets so my children could sleep there all night. They would sit there and watch cartoons and sometimes a scary movie.

While I was upstairs changing into my house clothes, I heard the doorbell ring. My mom yelled and said she got it. Then she called me downstairs. It was Rocky. In my mind, I was like, damn. My children were all awake. I didn't want them to see him, or him to see my children. Because, as he said, he was not ready for a relationship. He said he considered me a really good friend. I guess I was too much of an open book to him, plus I was giving up the cookies whenever he came to my home. It was an hour earlier than he would have normally come to my home. But I try to be honest with any man if I thought it was a possibility for a relationship. I did want him as my man: we had great conversations, great sex, he called me every day. My mom was asking him questions, and they were laughing and joking. So in my mind, there was a possibility we could move to the next level. He said hi to my children and they said hi to him. My mom and my kids had a cup of warm milk with cookies. We all sat down and watched television. Then they all fell asleep. Except for my mom, she was still watching television. They were watching VCR tapes. I did not have cable.

Then Rocky and I started to walk upstairs quietly. Mommy said good night to me and Rocky. We went into my room and had sex, then fell asleep. Mommy woke us up with pancakes, sausage, and eggs for breakfast. After he ate, he got dressed and left. I hurried up and changed the sheets on my bed and flipped my mattress over, then washed my ass. Then I got dressed, got out my children's clothes, and had them all wash-up, one by one. Then I opened the back door after I took the wood 4x4 off the door. The reason I had it on the back door is because whoever lived there before me put it there, so I kept it there. I felt safer with it there anyways. My children went outside to play while Mommy was talking to me, but all I was thinking about was Rocky. I really started to like him, but I knew not to like him too much. I always kept in mind what my male cousin said to me: What man would want a woman like me, who has a lot of kids?

Slowly but surely, Rocky and I drifted apart with our friendship. He admitted to me he had a woman and a new baby. Then he told me that he was about to get married soon. I left that dog alone; he never once told me that he was in a relationship.

*****

Months passed, and I was doing a lot better. Between taking my children to school, daycare, and working a part-time job, I met men, but none I really liked. Then one night, one guy I'd been chatting with for a while caught my attention. Also, I was seeing another guy while chatting with this one man. The rule I gave the man was never to call me after 8:00 pm because I'm in bed. I would say we'd been chatting on the phone for two months now, and we had long conversations. I was telling my friend next door about him.

I was even dating this other guy, well not dating—we were just sexually with one another. The relationship didn't last long because he wanted me to have his baby. He didn't have any children. A small part of me wanted to have his baby, but then we only went out once. I could only see him at certain times. That was when my children were at school or when they were asleep. So I didn't believe we would last long. After sleeping with him for two months now, my friend who introduced him to me said he was seeing another woman. She even told me that he got the woman pregnant. Wow, I knew not to trust him, even though the sex was good. I waited until the night he caught the bus to my house, right when he thought he was coming over to get some ass. I said "congratulations" to him as he came in the door.

He said, "For what?"

"I heard that you are about to become a new dad."

"He asked me, "Where did you hear this lie from?""

"Your best friend's wife told me."

"That lying bitch," he said.

"Oh really, she's lying?" I called her while he was there, and she and him were arguing on the phone. I said to him, "Get your lying ass out of my house."

As soon as he crossed the door, closed the door, while he was trying to say something to me, all of a sudden my phone rang. It was the man I'd been chatting with for two months. I hardly remember anything we talked about. But as we chatted that night, the conversation was very interesting. I don't know if I was paying him attention now because of what happened with me and Richie. But this man told me he would call me tomorrow after we'd been chatting on the phone for a while. I had to get up early anyway. I had work in the morning; I hadn't been at this new job long.

After work, I went to pick up my children, got some groceries, and cooked dinner. I got my babies ready for bed, then the phone rang. It was the man again. We chatted for a while, then all of a sudden, out of the blue, he invited me out to dinner and a movie. Wow, I got excited because a stranger is taking me on a date! He didn't ask to come over to my house and we didn't have any sex conversations. I answered him and said, "Yes, I can go out with you tomorrow." He said, "Okay, I will pick you up at 8:00."

So after getting off the phone with him, I called my mother and asked her if she could watch the kids. She said yes. I told her that I would drop them off at 5:00 pm tomorrow. I was off of work; even if I had to work, I didn't have any money or bus fare to get to work.

As soon as my babies went to bed, I went to my neighbor next door to me. I told her about the date I have tomorrow. She and I were both getting excited. I chatted with her for about 20 minutes. I couldn't wait to get back home so I could go to bed.

When the morning came, I was moving fast, but it seemed like time was moving slow. After I dropped my children off to school and daycare, I rushed home to see what I was going to wear. I didn't have many options. I didn't have that many clothes. I didn't know what to do to my hair; it was cut short and nappy. I wished I had money to get my hair done. I also wished I never cut my hair. I didn't want this man to see my short hair; he may not like me. I hoped he was cute. All these thoughts were going through my mind. Now all of a sudden time wanted to move fast. I needed to hurry up and pick my children up from school, and the baby from daycare. After picking them up, I called Mommy. She answered.

"Hey, Ma."

"What?" she said.

"Please, can you come to my house and watch my children?"

"With what bus fare? No, you bring them to my house," she said.

"I don't have any money to bring them."

So now it was 6:00 pm already. I was stressing about how to get my kids there. This man knew I have five children. So I called the man and told him that I couldn't go out tonight. He asked me why not.

"Because I don't have enough time to take my children to my mother's house," I said. I was lying. I didn't have bus fare, and I didn't want to tell him that I had no money. I'd never seen him before, and besides, I didn't know what type of man he was. We'd never seen what each other looked like.

He said to me, "It's okay, I can take you to drop the kids off to your mother's." Then he also said, "I really want to go out with you."

I said okay. I was so nervous and anxious. I called my friend next door and asked her to watch my children. She said, "Girl, bring your kids over here." I felt relief; I was afraid to put my children in a stranger's car. After I finished feeding my kids dinner, helped them with their homework, and made them change their clothes into their play clothes, I walked next door and dropped them off. Now I only had 30 minutes to get ready.

It was 7:30 pm. I had to hurry up and take a shower, get my clothes on, and do something with my short hair. I ended up wearing my black flat shoes and my red and black ankle-length skirt with a black shirt. I wrapped my scarf on my head with a bun on the back after I slicked my hair down with gel. It was now 8:05 and my phone rang.

The man said, "I'm outside in a brown truck."

My heart was beating so fast. I called my friend and said, "I'm leaving now," just in case she wanted to peep out the window. I then locked my door and walked out towards his truck. I was so nervous with this big Kool-Aid smile on my face.

As soon as I got close to his truck, he said "Natasha," and I responded "Rudopho." I then walked around to the passenger side. As soon as I entered the truck I noticed his gas light was on. He said hi to me. I said hello. I was still nervous. This was my first time seeing him.

"Where are your children? I thought you wanted me to drop them off to your mother's house."

I said, "No, it's okay, thank you anyway. They are at my friend's house."

Rudopho responded, "Okay."

I then said, "Your gas is low. Are you going to get some gas?"

He said yes. I had my hand on the door handle just in case I had to run out. Because now he did make a mistake and turned down two different dead-end streets. These are some rough areas.

"Do you know where you are going?"

He did not respond to me. Finally, we got to the gas station. From there, he took me to the movies. I was so tired, I fell asleep a couple of times in the movie. Then he woke me up. When we left, he took me to a Spanish restaurant, and we had a nice, clean conversation. Me, I was talking about my beautiful children and about my job. After eating, he then brought me home.

Before I exited the car, I said, "I had a nice time, Rudopho. Hopefully, I'll see you again." I felt good. He didn't try to get any ass from me, wow. He was a very attractive man and had a nice personality.

I went straight to my friend's house and picked up my children. She asked me to call her when I got in the house. She wanted to know how the date went as well. I couldn't wait to see the man again. Rudopho and I chatted on the phone almost every night. We ended up going on another date a week later, same day, same time. Same thing: dinner and a movie.

On the third date, I took the bus to my mom's and dropped the children off and hurried back home. After running downtown to the store, I went and bought myself some new underwear, jeans, and a shirt. On this third date, he took me to dinner and back to his house. He lived in North Newark. I was so nervous at his house. He was soft-spoken and handsome. While we were at his house, I tried to keep my conversation clean. I sat at the opposite end of his futon. When I had to go to the bathroom, I saw on his floor so many porn videos, but I didn't say anything about it. I came back out of the bathroom and sat down. We were both sitting there watching a movie and having a light conversation, then he sat closer to me.

After that movie went off, he poured me another drink and one for himself. He got up and popped porn in the DVD player. I clenched my thighs together. I had to try my hardest to be good. He was sitting there smiling and smoking a cigar, watching the movie. I felt so uncomfortable. I started getting horny. Damn, I tried. Next thing I know, he started kissing me. I was kissing him back. He grabbed my hand and put my hands in his pants. I liked what I was feeling; it made me more excited. Next thing I knew, my pants and panties were down to my ankles, and we were against the wall. He put on a hat and stuck it in. Damn, this shit feels so good, we went from the wall to the futon. I then started riding him, then we went into doggie style.

Next thing I knew, it was the next morning. While he was asleep, I put my clothes on, then walked down the street to the store. I bought breakfast to cook for me and him. What I bought was pancake mix, bacon, eggs, and orange juice. Then I cooked breakfast for me and him. After we ate breakfast, we both took a separate shower and got dressed. Then he asked me if I wanted to go to the pier at Jersey City. I said sure. I wore the same clothes I had on. While we were riding to Jersey City, we were stuck in traffic. He was bopping me in the head with his water bottle.

"Stop it, please. I don't play those hitting games." He apologized and for the fourth time, he bopped my head with the water bottle. I then opened my water bottle and threw the water in his face. "I told you I don't play hitting games."

I could tell he was upset with me. But I didn't want to start with those hitting games, for fear it may turn into him whooping my ass later on down the line. The traffic started moving, and we were almost to our destination. He got off the highway and drove on the streets for about 25 minutes, then parked the car.

"Come on, let's go," he said.

"I don't see no water," I replied.

He said, "We have to walk. It's around the corner."

I got out of the car, and he came over to me and held my hand briefly. I was smiling from ear to ear. We walked all around Exchange Place by the water. From there we grabbed a bite to eat at one of those food trucks. We talked about a lot of things. This time he was doing most of the talking. I really enjoyed my time out with him. We hung out in Exchange Place for almost the whole day. When we got back to his truck, Rudopho asked me to come back to his place. I didn't mind going back to his place. I bought myself another outfit at a discounted price, more underwear; I was ready.

On our way to his house, we stopped at a restaurant to pick up dinner to bring back to his place. We watched a movie, then we had sex again; not like the night before, it was a quickie. My nose was wide open. Yes, I liked this man for real. The next morning, which was Sunday, he brought me to my mom's house to pick up my children. I ran upstairs to my mom's house and picked my babies up, and we all got into his truck. Then he dropped us off to my home.

Every weekend, I was with him. My children were at my mother's house, but most of the time she came to my house. He introduced me to his two children on two different occasions. One of his children did not like me because I had five children. She would have an attitude and talk rudely to me and about me. But I ignored it, being she was a child. I talked with her and said it was not my place to take her dad away from her. Anytime she wanted to see him it was up to him and her. I would never get in between her and her dad, that it was not my place.

Rudopho and I were busy together every weekend. We went out to different places. I introduced him to some of my friends. We would go to their houses and play spades, drink, and listen to music. One of my friends that he met at the spades game, invited us to her meet and greet party later on that night. Rudopho said sure we can go. I was surprised when he agreed to go to the party. I didn't think he knew what a meet and greet was, or maybe he did know what type of party it was. After we finished playing spades, Rudopho and I left. I wanted to go home and get something nice and sexy to wear. When Rudopho was driving me home, I had him stop at the store. I went inside to buy two boxes of condoms and went next door to the liquor store to get two bottles of alcohol. In order to get into the party, everyone had to bring drinks and condoms. I got into the car and he drove me to my house. He came into the house with me and he sat on the couch.

I ran upstairs to get in the shower so I could get dressed. We only had a couple of hours to get to the party. As soon as I got in the shower, I started washing my short hair. My eyes were closed and I felt someone behind me, rubbing on me. While the soap was still in my hair, as I was washing it out, he started having sex with me. We were enjoying one another for a while. Then we finished washing our bodies and then we got dressed. I wanted to look hot and sexy and make Rudopho more excited. I got out of the shower and dried myself off and lotioned myself up. I then put on my short black skirt and a black shirt that had a bra attached to it. I tied it up behind my neck. I then put on my red high heels and my crotchless stockings.

We both left and headed to the party in Edison. He kept looking at me, smiling, and talking about what he was going to do to me after the party. As soon as we got to Darlei's house, the friend at a meet and greet party opened the door to let us in. We all had to buy a box of condoms and drop it in the bowl. I didn't say anything to him about it, because I didn't know if he liked stuff like this. Rudopho and I went and sat at the table in the dining room. We were all in the house chilling, listening to music, and holding a conversation. The meet and greet was for one hour, and the swing started right after. I was sitting at the table, trying to look sexy. I had to behave myself while sitting next to my man. Well, he was not my man yet, but I sure was claiming it.

This girl Candy came into the house and headed towards me. I remembered her from the last swing. She was caramel, tall, and thick, with green eyes and shoulder-length hair. She stood in front of me and said "get up," and held my hand to help me up. Candy then sat down in my seat and pulled me on her lap. Next thing I know, she started rubbing my breast for a little and Rudopho's eyes got big. Then she pulled my breast out and was about to put it into her mouth. I was getting excited, but I had to stop her. I also wanted Rudopho to make the first move if he was down with the swinging lifestyle. I asked him if he was okay. He said yes, but he was ready to leave. So after I finished my drink and said my goodbyes to everyone, we left the party. I didn't want to go. I got hot in the pants with excitement, but I had to be good.

When he and I got in the car, I was feeling nice from all those drinks. I was talking very fresh to Rudopho, even touching myself. He pulled over to the side of some dark alleyway and we had a quickie in the truck. As soon as we finished, he drove straight to his home and we had more sex. This time, sex was more fun. He let me pull out my handcuffs and blindfold. I then cuffed his one hand, since he did not feel too comfortable with the cuffs. I then undressed him and cuffed his arm to the futon. I put on the blindfold, and he kept calling me, asking me what I was doing.

"I'm right here, baby. I am not going nowhere." I then went down on my knees and started kissing him from his neck, working my way down to my joystick. I started kissing and teasing him. He got so excited, he took the cuff off and the blindfold, and he took control. I was not finished with what I wanted to do to him, but he was ready. He fucked me so hard, so long, then he pulled me on top of him and I rode that horse like it was no tomorrow. That was a good night. We both had to catch our breath.

Anyway, we were on month three in our dating. I now had my own roadmaster station wagon. He got to meet my dad. He even met me at the park on his early days to hang out with me and my children, and on some Saturday afternoons, he went with me and my children to different events. I was still working part-time, looking for a fulltime job.

Every time I introduced Rudopho to everyone, I introduced him as my man. He used to ask me why I kept telling people he is my man. I said, "Because you act as if you are my man. We go out every weekend and we help each other out. I wash your clothes when I wash mines and my children's clothes. I fix your plate and you come to my home to pick it up. I even let you meet my children. So, you my man." And I smiled.

He didn't say anything much, except that we were still in the dating phase. Okay, sure, if you say so. This one Saturday night, he invited me to the bar. I was happy. I never went out this much with a man. I was used to being in the bed all the time with a man. When Friday came, I went to pick my mom up and brought her to my house so she could watch the kids for the weekend. I picked the kids up from school. I cooked dinner, pulled out some movies for them to watch with their grandma, I gave all of them a hug and a kiss, and said see you later. I drove to Rudopho's house, and we just watched television, ate dinner that he cooked, had sex, and went to bed.

On Saturday morning, we just cleaned up his place, got dressed, and went to his friend's house. His friend made a joke about their age compared to my age.

When he said, "She hangs around a bunch of old heads," then his friend asked me my age. I replied 29 years old, and he said jokingly, "How you ended up with an old man like him?"

I said, "He's only 34, that's not old."

He laughed at me and said, "More like 45."

So, I sat there, counting by my fingers under the table. Wow, he's 16 years older than me. Okay, so he lied about his age. I still liked him anyway. Later that night, we left his friend's home in New York. We went to some bar in Edison, New Jersey.

After my second drink, I wrote on a paper and gave it to Rudopho: *You are going to end up being my husband.*

He said, "Get out of here. What are you drinking?"

I said, "I'm not drunk. I see it. I see that you are going to marry me."

He said, "Something is wrong with you. You are crazy." He then said, "No, because I'm not going to get married. I barely know you."

I responded, "Okay, I won't say nothing else, but watch it come to pass." I guess it was that liquor in me had me feeling some type of way.

Then he told me that he was still sleeping with his ex-girl. He said they were not in a relationship, but he was sleeping with her.

"Wow, you picked a fine time to tell me." I didn't even bother to get upset. Like he said, we were only dating.

When we got towards the end of the fourth month of dating, we alternated between me staying at his house and him staying at my place. I sometimes used to just pop up at his place just to get a quickie, where I just dropped my pants to my ankles and he did me doggie style. We used to have sex everywhere or anywhere when we would be out. I sometimes wore a skirt with no panties on for easy access. Our sex life was very fun and enjoyable. He was not a foreplay type of guy; something I had to get used to, I guess. I didn't complain, because I liked him a lot; I didn't want to mess up what we had. He kept me busy and we went out a lot. We even started going places with my children. My children would have fun at the places we would go. We took them to movies, museums, and amusement parks. It was like the daytime we spent with my children, and the nighttime was for me and him.

*****

School was out, and it was now summer vacation. I was still working my part-time job. Some weekends, Rudopho would invite me and my children to grill out at one of the parks. I would respond yes, then we would go to the grocery store. I tried not to hurt his pockets when we went shopping, so I was picking up cheap, low-priced items I knew my children would eat. He was picking up name-brand everything. When we got to the checkout line, I started putting the items on the counter. He picked up a magazine and started reading it. The cashier said the total was $113.00. Me, I am on a budget. I don't have much money to spare. I only had my bill money. The lady said the price again, so I cleared my throat loudly to get his attention. He did not lift up his head, so I cleared my throat again. Still no response from him. (I wanted to yell at him, "I know you hear the lady, acting like you so into that magazine.") So, I then reached into my wallet and paid the bill. That's when he all of a sudden put the magazine down and picked up the bags. In my head, I was stressing about how I was going to pay my cellular phone bill.

That was the second time he did that to me.

When he asked me a third time to grill out, I straight up asked him, "Are you going half on the bill, or paying for the whole thing?"

He replied, "I will go half," then he reached into his wallet and gave me $30.00.

I said, "Okay, you need to watch what you get. I cannot afford to spare no more than $30.00 either." He said okay, and we got less food that time. We bought bologna, cheese, beverages, bread, and chips. That was all. We watched the children running around, playing, and having fun. We all sat down and ate, then everyone got into the truck. He dropped me and my children off home. I had to give my babies a bath. They had too much fun; they got so dirty.

Rudopho told me he would be leaving later that day. He and his daughters were taking a one-week vacation to Florida. He came by my place and stayed for a little while and watched television with me and my babies before he got on the road. When he was ready to leave, I gave him a Bible. He thanked me and said he would see me as soon as he got back from Florida. I was going to miss Rudopho. I hoped the week went by very fast. When he got to his mother's house the next day, he called me to let me know that he made it there safely. I was excited to hear from him. We chatted for about five minutes, then he said he would call me later.

During that week, I took my children to the park, skating, swimming, etc. I took them to their summer program on the days I had to go to work. I was doing lots of things to stay busy and to keep out of trouble. I was very determined to work hard the safe way and to stay off my back in other men's beds or hotels to make money.

He called me every day to check up on me. Finally, the week went by and he came to see me the next day. The first thing he did when he popped up to my place later that evening, was he kissed me. Then he said that he loved me, and he then said the words, "Let's get married."

"What?"

"You heard me, let's get married."

I had to rub it in. "I told you that you were going to ask me to marry you." I said, "Yes," hugging him so tight. I was excited because I had prayed for a husband.

That very next day we started making and setting dates. I wanted to get married next month in August, but he said, "No, let's do it in September."

I said, "Okay, the first Saturday of September."

"He said, "No, September the 10th."

I said, "No, that's my son's birthday."

We both agreed to October the 9th, then we decided to go to the store. We were looking for do-it-yourself wedding invitations. It was becoming very stressful planning a wedding on a budget. Rudopho and I were having a lot of disagreements with the way we wanted the wedding to be. I called my sisters and brothers, cousins, and friends and told them about my wedding date. Some of them were negative, saying: so soon, so fast. One brought up my first marriage. "You remember you married your first husband only knowing him for three months."

I said, "Okay, well love doesn't know the time. And besides, we will be together for six months on our wedding day."

He called his family. I was excited, very excited. I had my own man, soon to be my husband. My sisters and I were making plans and talking about the decorations. I was out shopping and looking for my children's outfits. Then Rudopho and I had to go to City Hall to get our marriage license with two witnesses. From there, I went to the store and ordered food for the wedding. I was so scared to ask him for money to help pay for the wedding. I didn't want to mess things up between us. I was working overtime at my job, and every penny I got, I was saving it for my wedding. I'd never had a church wedding before. We rented a hall for a great price, and the Pastor who knew my husband and my cousin said to just give him a small donation. The Pastor was doing our wedding basically for nothing.

We had one week before my wedding. I got sick. I was not feeling well. My teeth were acting up and my stomach was upset. Rudopho was now staying with me at my place. He moved in with me two weeks before our wedding. Anyway, I was feeling really bad and didn't get out of bed. He left out the house early in the morning, and when he came back in the house, he came upstairs in our bedroom and started yelling. I was tired, so I sat up and said, "What?"

He started yelling again. "You nasty, your kids are nasty, this house is nasty."

I said, "Why you say that?"

He said, "The house is fucking nasty. You let your kids dirty up the fucking house."

I said, "First of all, if the house is dirty, why didn't you ask the kids to clean up?"

He said, "They aren't my kids."

Now I was angry. I started yelling back at him. "How the fuck is you about to marry me and scared to ask my kids to clean up? You see I don't feel good, and the house is always clean. My oldest daughter had to fix breakfast for her and her siblings. I couldn't get out of bed. I did not know that they made a mess downstairs."

"The wedding is off," he said.

I said, "Okay, your ass don't got to say it no more. Wedding off. Good."

Now I was upset. I called my sisters in Virginia. "Hey D, don't come. Wedding off." I called my other sister. "Hey, Lutie, don't come. Wedding off." Click.

As soon as I started to call my dad, he grabbed the phone from me. "I'm sorry," he said. "I was being an asshole. Don't tell your dad. Don't call anyone else. I love you and I want you to be my wife."

I said, "It's okay. I'm good. Next time you need to talk to me instead of yelling at me. I have feelings, you know. We don't have to get married. I told you, and you know that I have five children. Kids make messes, especially when I'm in the bed not feeling well. But you could have said something to them before it turned into a mess."

Next thing I know, he said we're still having the wedding on that date.

I said, "Are you sure?" He said yes.

After he put his things down, he went downstairs to clean up, and he asked my babies to help him nicely. I didn't get out of bed until later that night. I was so sick and was not feeling well. He stayed out of the bedroom all day. He and my children were watching cartoons.

The next day, we took my children to the park and to see the water by the Exchange Place in Jersey City. We grabbed food to eat in the car and went home later that night. I gave my children a bath and got them ready for bed. I made sure the house was clean and got my butt in the bed. I had to go to work tomorrow.

When I got to work, me and two of my friends were talking about my wedding coming up. I gave them an invitation to my wedding. After work, I got in my car and smoked a cigarette, a filthy habit I'd picked back up. In the past, I smoked one day or a couple of days and quit. But this time, I was smoking a half a pack a day, depending upon my stress level. I was excited, nervous, anxious, afraid, and was having second thoughts. I prayed that this feeling would go away. I prayed he is my happily ever after. Like those movies I watched coming up from a child.

I was almost finished buying my children's clothes for the wedding. I started my car and was heading to downtown Newark to buy my wedding dress. I went to a couple of stores, then at the 3rd store, I found the dress. I didn't really like the dress. I only liked that the color was baby-powder blue. I didn't want to get married in royal blue again. The dress was also long to my feet and came with a sheer scarf. I wished this dress had a little sleeve on it, but it was shoestring straps. I brought the dress to the counter and paid the cashier the $110.00 for my dress. Then from there, I went to Payless and got me a pair of low heel baby-powder blue strap heels. I ran home first to drop off my clothes.

While I was putting my dress in the closet, I heard the doorbell. Not knowing who it could be, I ran downstairs. As soon as I opened the door, it was the guy I dated briefly who got some girl pregnant. He pushed himself in my door, crying and upset. He was asking me why I was doing it.

"Doing what?"

"Why are you getting married?"

"Because I am in love."

He had the nerve to say he loves me.

"If you loved me, you would not get some other girl pregnant."

He would not leave out my house, so I rushed to the kitchen to put the clothes I had washing in the dryer. I turned around, and he was right there. He grabbed me, hugging me tight, saying he loves me. I was pushing him off of me, and next thing I knew, he lifted me and sat me on the washing machine. He hugged me some more, then he worked his way down between my legs. He started kissing on my valley below. I tried to stop him, but my arms grew weak with pleasure. I never experienced a man crying and kissing me at the same time.

"Stop it, you have to stop," I was speaking in a soft tone.

He would not stop, so I pushed him off me.

"I have to pick my children up and you need to go. My fiancé will be home soon. Please stop."

As soon as he got off of me and out of my house, I rushed out to pick up my children from day camp and my baby from daycare. I went to the store to get my lottery ticket and a bottle of wine. As soon as I parked in the parking lot, my children got out of the car to go in the store. After getting my children a snack and my stuff, we left out of the store. As soon as my babies and I came out of the store, a car came speeding in the parking lot. This car almost hit my son.

I yelled, "Hey, you almost hit my son."

He had the nerve to say my son should not have been in the way. So I hurried and got my kids in the car and waited outside for him. I was upset with his response. As soon as he stepped out the door, I sped in front of him in my car.

He jumped out of my way and yelled, "You crazy bitch, you almost hit me."

I yelled back at him, "You shouldn't have been in my way." I wasn't going to hit him, but I wanted to scare his ass like he scared me. He was very close to my son with his car.

From there, I took my children to the park for a little while. Besides, I had to calm my nerves down. We stayed at the park for about an hour. I had to leave the park to go home to clean and cook dinner.

I was excited thinking about my sisters; they would be here in three days. We were supposed to go shopping for the table decorations and other things for the wedding. One sister said she was going to treat me to a pedicure and manicure. The other sister said we were going out to party the night before the wedding. I was excited. The days were going by fast, and I didn't get my hair done yet. I'd just been slicking my hair into a ponytail. I'd never met my fiancé's family. I hoped that they liked me, and accepted me and my five children. I was really nervous.

*****

I took the day off of work, because it was only one more day until my wedding, and my sisters came to New Jersey last night. She stopped by my house after she checked into the hotel. She wanted me to try on the wedding dress. So I ran upstairs to my room and put it on. She and my fiancé were downstairs waiting. I came downstairs with the dress on, and she had this look on her face.

She said, "I know you're not going to wear this dress," in a soft-spoken tone.

Then my fiancé added his two cents to the conversation. He had the nerve to say, "I'm trying to tell her."

"Tell me what?" I asked him.

My sister said, "Your arms."

"What's wrong with my arms?"

"It's big and doesn't look right with that dress."

I started to feel unsexy because my fiancé did a little laugh. I hurried upstairs and took off the dress.

Me and my sisters had to hurry and go shopping. I only had $300.00 left. I spent most of my money on the wedding. I didn't want to ask my future husband for nothing. He only had to pay for the cameraman, whatever he was wearing, and put the $200.00 deposit down for the hall. I paid for everything else: the food, the decorations, me and my children's clothes, and the donation to the pastor.

Before my sisters and I went shopping, I was looking in all the children's stores, trying to find a dress for my daughter. I had a hard time finding her dress. Then my mother happened to call me, and I told her I couldn't find my oldest child a dress. She said that she had a new dress that my oldest daughter can wear. She told me it was a cream-colored dress. I had no choice but to accept the dress.

"Thanks, mom," I replied. "I really wanted a baby-powder blue dress for her so all my children can match me. I will pick it up later on tonight."

Time was moving so fast; I didn't even go shopping yet for the decorations.

"Let's hurry up and get your feet and nails done before the nail salon close," my sister said to me. "We will go shopping afterward." My neighbor was watching my children for me, so I had plenty of time.

Anyway, when I got into the salon, I had to pick a color for my feet and nails. The woman asked me to take my shoes off and put my feet in the water. I was feeling so excited because I'd never had a pedicure before. I'd only had manicures. When the lady took my feet out of the water, she clipped my nails, buffed it, and started scrubbing it. I was getting so excited, it was feeling so good. I was smiling so hard, squeezing my thighs together. Am I supposed to feel like this? Let me talk to my sister and think about something else. This pedicure felt so good, it was like it took my stress away. My sister was smiling at me; me smiling back. I had to thank her for this pedicure. After that I got my nails done, and then the lady waxed my eyebrows.

From there, we went to the bargain store and I got the decorations for the table, the decorated paper plates and cups, and balloons. Everything was baby-powder blue and white, even the plastic tablecloth. After we got everything I needed for the wedding, we went to my mom's house to pick up the dress for my daughter. We sat and chatted with my mom for a while. My sisters and I were tired and agreed to go out some other day. We were too tired to do anything else.

After my sister dropped me off to my house, I left the decorations in my sister's car, since my baby sister was doing the decorations. I picked my children up from next door and bathed them all, then straight to bed they went. I didn't have to cook since they ate dinner at my friend's house. I didn't see or hear from my fiancé all day. I guess I would see him tomorrow at noon. Since I didn't go out and party tonight, I just went to bed.

The next morning, I heard my fiancé saying, "Oh, she's home. We got to go somewhere else to get dressed." Then he left.

I hurried up and got in the shower, then got my children dressed. From there, I jumped in my car to look for a salon to do my hair. It was now 10:00 am. I was panicking now. The first salon said by appointment only; the other salon said I had to come back at noon. I was so worried that I was going to be late for my wedding. Then I went to the braiding salon, and the lady said she only do braids. So I had to get two cornrows in my hair because now it was 11:30 am. As soon as she finished, I had to rush home with my children. Then I washed up again from sweating and got dressed. Then I called me a taxi.

My phone was ringing off the hook. Three people called me, asking me where I was. I replied to everyone: "I'm close," or "I'm on my way." My taxi came at 12:30; he had to drive me from Bergen Street to Orange, New Jersey. By the time I got out of the taxi, I saw these women standing at the door. I was nervous. I felt very unattractive. I wanted to get a hairstyle to cover my big forehead, but it didn't go as planned.

As soon as I walked to the church steps, one of the ladies said, "There she is." I didn't know who they were. One said, "Oh, she is pretty," and they all started hugging me. One lady said for me to go downstairs; the other said, "No, stay right there. Your husband is already standing, waiting."

Then Daddy came out and said when the music comes on, he was going to walk me in after my baby put down the flowers. My baby girl was the flower girl.

As soon as the music started playing, I said, "Go ahead baby, walk in and start dropping the flowers."

She walked in and ran back out. She was crying, saying, "Mommy, I'm scared."

So my mother came and picked her up, and she started dropping down the rose petals. Then Daddy and I walked in to the gospel song I chose. I was so nervous; everyone was looking at me. My husband and I didn't even have any wedding rehearsal. So I didn't know what I was doing or what to expect. It seemed so fast. We repeated the vows after the pastor. My sister, who was my bridesmaid, passed us the rings. Then all I remember is the Pastor said, "You may kiss your bride." I was excited and closed my eyes. I was ready for that wedding kiss that you see in the movies. My husband just pecked me on the lips and grabbed my hand. (What, that was it? That was not the kiss I was looking for in my mind.) I guess he was nervous too.

We walked straight out of the church to the hallway where the pastor met us. I then gave him the deposit, the last of what I had, $100.00. From there, the people started gathering around us to hug and congratulate us. The women who were standing in front of the door as I was coming in introduced themselves. One was my husband's mom, cousin, and aunt. After we all finished talking, my husband and I said we would meet everyone at the hall. My sister took my kids with her to the hall. Me and my now-husband Rudopho went to the supermarket to pick up the food I ordered. From there, we drove to the hall.

When we got to the hall, we started to bring in the food, and some of the people helped us. We had about 50 people at our wedding. It looked so beautiful. My sisters did an excellent job in decorating. I was so excited. Then my husband set up his computer to the speakers and he was playing music. I didn't dance because I was disappointed. I wanted to hire a DJ, but my husband convinced me not to waste money on a DJ.

As my husband was playing music, some people asked me to dance. I said no thank you. So his mother got up to dance with him. And some other people were dancing. But me, I walked around and talked with my family, then went to the other room to get a drink from the bar. As soon as I sat at the bar, I ordered a drink. I was grateful my cousin paid for my drink; she said it was my wedding day and I shouldn't have to pay. After we finished eating and we cut the cake, some of the people helped us clean up, and then people left with plates. There was plenty of food left. I wanted to get rid of all the food. My mother-in-law cut a piece of the cake, and she said to leave it in the freezer for one year.

When everyone left, so did we. We went home, and I changed my children's clothes to their play clothes. I left out of the house to go take my children to my mom's house so she could watch my babies. As soon as I got to her house, I knocked on her door. She wouldn't let me in.

"Ma, you promised me that you will watch the kids."

She said, "No, come back tomorrow."

"Please, Ma. Watch my babies. It's my wedding night."

"No!" And she slammed the door in my face.

I was upset with her, but I was not going to let my night be ruined. My children and I got in the car, and my husband was not too happy when I came back home with my children. So I stayed downstairs and fed my babies, got their pajamas on, read them a story, and put them to bed.

Then I put on my sexy lingerie in the bathroom after I showered, went downstairs, and got the bottle of wine and two wine glasses, my CD, and candles. I wanted to give my husband all my attention sexually.

So I came into the room, lit the four candles, put on my oldies but goodies, and poured me and him a glass of wine. He was laying in the bed with his back towards me. I started to kiss him.

"Leave me alone, I got a headache," he said to me.

I said, "The kids are asleep and it's our wedding night."

"Leave me alone and blow out those candles. That's how house fires start."

My feelings were crushed. I went downstairs in the living room and drank the wine by myself and listened to the music in the dimly lit room. It bothered me emotionally that he did not want to be bothered with me.

The next morning, I woke up on the couch and fed my children breakfast. I drove to my mother's house, and she said she would watch my children. From there, I picked up my husband and took him out to the hotel in Atlantic City. Thank God some of the people gave money as a gift. We ate and finally had sex at the hotel later that night. It was not that honeymoon experience I would have liked to have had; it was a quickie. But we had sex, finally.

We left the next morning because I had to work. When I got to the job, my supervisor sent me home early. She also cut back my hours to two days a week. That wasn't enough money to support my family. So, when I went home I started applying for jobs. Yes, two jobs hired me; they were both part-time cashier jobs.

I was working so many hours to support my family. My work hours were causing a lot of problems at home. My husband said that I had to cut back on my hours because he got himself another job too, and that he couldn't be watching my kids. He only had to watch them at night because they were in a summer day camp in the day until 5:00 pm. I used to get off work at midnight. I got home by 12:30. I only worked four nights until midnight. The day job was only three days. So, after working both jobs for a couple of weeks, my husband asked me to go back to school. So, I had to quit my day job and keep my night job. I ended up going to school for medical services. Then one day I saw a job opening for public transportation. In between work, school, and home life, I sure was very busy.

*****

It was five months into my marriage, and I missed the first two weeks of my marriage when Rudopho used to hold my hands and open the doors for me. I felt like a woman. Now I had to hold the door open for myself, and I had to keep myself together, like keep my hair done and wear sexy-fitting clothes just to receive compliments from other people. I wished I received compliments from Rudopho; he was becoming a mean-ass. He was very rude towards me. I wished he had shown me this side of him before we got married. He was always making fat jokes and giving me this look like he regrets getting married. I hated to even walk past him naked, the mean shit he would say.

Today is my birthday. I am now 30 years old. My husband left out of the house at 5:00 am. When he got home, he handed me a small birthday cake and card. I said, "Thank you, and you were gone all day."

He replied that he went for a jog and then he went to the store.

"It took you all of six hours, wow."

He stuck his hand in his pocket and said, "No, I was not gone that long."

"Okay," I said, "whatever."

As Rudopho pulled his hand out of his pocket, something brown fell to the floor. I got out of bed and looked. He was walking down the stairs.

"Rudopho."

"What?" he answered.

"You dropped something."

"What?" he said.

"On the floor."

"What is it?"

"Come look and see."

He came back up to look. He picked them up and put it back in his pocket.

"Whose are those? I know it's not yours. Who are those female panties? I know it's not mine. My ass too big to get in those brown panties."

He said they were old; he had them for a long time; it probably got mixed up in his clothes.

"How, when I do your laundry and I always check the pockets?" He ignored me and walked away. I yelled at him, "Why was the vagina seat wet in those panties?"

He came right back in the room, after hearing me digging through his things. "What the fuck are you doing?" Rudopho asked me.

"I'm looking for more panties I might have missed."

He said, "Sit down, please. I need to talk to you."

I was yelling and fussing, looking for some more panties. "About what do you need to talk to me about, Rudopho?"

"Promise me you won't get upset," said Rudopho.

"I can't promise, but I am listening."

"Promise me."

"Okay, whatever. I promise."

"I made a mistake."

"What did you make a mistake with, Rudopho? Please tell me."

"I have been seeing someone."

"Seeing them how, and who is it?"

"I am not going to tell you, but it's over now."

"What are you telling me, Rudopho? Please tell me what you are talking about."

"I made a mistake and had sex with my ex-girl this morning."

"Wow, how long this been going on, Rudopho?"

"It doesn't matter. It's all over now. You are who I want and need."

"Wow, I can't believe what I'm hearing. What is wrong with me that you have to go outside of our marriage?" Tears started rolling down my face. "I can't believe you. So, did you see her the night before our wedding? Is that why you did not want to sleep with me, Rudopho?"

"No, I was upset that your mom couldn't watch the children so we could be alone together."

"The lies you tell. I can't believe this." I wanted to be really upset with him, but I couldn't after what had happened on top of my washing machine. "I hope and pray you are really done messing with whoever this person is."

He came up to me and was hugging me and kissing me, apologizing to me. We ended up laying in the bed for a while, not saying anything to one another. Me, I was heavy in thought, wondering will my marriage last? Will we be able to stay together?

After a little time passed, I got up and took my children to the park for a while, then we came home and I cooked dinner and got them ready for bed. I went into the room and tried to have intimacy with my husband. It had now been two weeks.

"I have a headache, leave me alone."

I tried again the next night. "I have a headache."

I said, "Okay, I will try again next week."

After dropping my children off to school, I got a call back from transportation, asking me to come in and take the test and a physical. I was so excited. I got my GED and was in medical school, and would soon be driving the bus. I had to go to the department and take a test and fill out all kinds of paperwork. I was thinking to myself, I really can take care of my children.

One week later, I got a call: "You passed the test. You have to do training for two weeks. 8:00 am to 4:00 pm. The training is paid," the lady said.

"Thank you, I can't wait to tell everyone the good news." I hung up the phone so fast after saying, "See you Monday," to the lady.

I hurried home and started dinner, picked up my kids from day camp, and called my husband and told him the good news.

"What are you going to do about medical school?"

"I am going to drop out," I said.

He didn't seem too happy with me dropping out of school. But the struggle was hard for me. I had to pay bills because it was my apartment. Buy my kids clothes—they were growing fast. Repair my car— didn't have enough to do it all— and it was hard just to keep gas in the car. Every time I asked him for money, his response would be "They are not my kids," or if I asked for money in general, he never had any to spare.

We even argued over the bills and money. He would ask me, "Whose name the bills are in?"

I responded, "My bills."

Then he'd say, "That's who should pay the bills."

I couldn't believe what I was hearing, but then again, I can. I had to tell him, "Look, you knew I had these five children before you married me. YOU KNEW I HAD THESE BILLS; YOU KNEW MY SITUATION. I did not put a gun to your head and say 'marry me.' If you don't want to be married, you can leave me; we can get a divorce."

We even argued over sex. He knew I liked sex, and every time I tried to get sex, he got a headache, he doesn't feel good, or he locked his penis between his thighs just so I couldn't touch it.

Then one day he decided to buy my children's clothes, so we went to some cheap store. He picked out some sweatsuits that were way too small for my children, or too big. But I couldn't complain; it was a start, I guess. He didn't have to do it.

*****

I went and bought sexy red lingerie for Valentine's day, some three-inch high heels, and a sexy wig, and I bought him some flowers. He looked at me and smiled really hard like he wanted to laugh.

He said, "Go to bed, it's late. I have to work in the morning."

I responded, "I am not tired, and I want some sex. It's been a while since we had sex."

He replied, "Go ahead and ride it. I am not doing nothing."

I turned the lights off and played my mood music. I went and started kissing on him, while he was just lying there.

"Just hurry up and do what you going to do already," he said to me.

So I then got on top of him and started riding. I was riding him so long and in many different positions I could think of. I wanted to excite him. He then said, "Damn, you fuck like a bitch who just got out of jail."

I felt like a fool, being he was not responding the way I hoped he would. Our sex life went from one time a week, to once every two weeks. Then, if we would have sex, he would say he had to put his mood music on, which was porn, and he had to have his drunk juice almost every time. I was cool with it for a while, at least I was getting sex. But after time went by, when I sat there and thought about it, I started feeling like I was not satisfying him. I was feeling like he was not attracted or turned on by me. I was also wondering if he was still fucking this woman. I had to say something to him.

"Rudopho, why every time we have sex you have to have porn and liquor? Is it because of my body or my weight? This hurts me, that you have to have these items every time now. I like slow jams as my mood music, not porn." Then we would argue about that. I said, "I don't care if you watch porn once in a blue, but all the time is too much. I already have a complex from the fat jokes you like to make."

It was becoming hard to try to please my husband sexually. I was trying to do everything I could think of to excite him. I even asked him what he would like me to change. I was at the point I was willing to change. I wanted to make him happy and keep him satisfied. I kept my hair done, nails done, and dressed sexy all the time, sometimes too sexy. I was buying new underwear every paycheck. It got to the point where I stopped complaining for a while and let him watch his movies while having sex with me. I would just stay very quiet so he could hear those women on the television. But deep down inside, it was bothering me.

I started venting to my friends, and all one friend did was shove weed in my face. She said I was stressing too much over nothing. My family didn't know what was wrong with me.

I even started snooping around. I found porn everywhere: on the computer, in the closet, in the car, on his phone. I used to sneak up in the middle of the night and find him watching porn in the basement with his dick in his hands. I would argue with him and ask, "Why do you have to sneak around watching porn?"

When I say we were having sex, it was only one time every two to three weeks. What is wrong with him, when we have a bedroom? The other argument was, "Why are you doing this when you could be sleeping with me?" I didn't understand why he'd rather touch himself instead of me. I was always ready for sex, no matter the time or how tired I would be; the word "no" would never be in my vocabulary.

I had never experienced a relationship like this. I was then getting worried, and ready for a divorce. I started questioning, "Why are you with me? What do you want from me?"

I would have all kinds of crazy thoughts in my mind. I started questioning my kids daily, asking if he touched them. They would say "no" in a disgusted way. "Please tell Mommy if he touched you because Mommy is crazy and she will fuck him up." I even asked my kids in front of him, to show my children not to have fear of this man who is my husband. I had to show my children Mommy got their back no matter what, and that I will protect them always to the best of my ability. It was even getting to the point where I told my children to stay away from him and had my oldest to keep an eye on him. I was worried every day I left them with him. But he sensed it and stayed out of the house until it was almost time for me to come home.

I now realize my husband Rudopho had a heavy porn addiction. We'd go on dates, and I'd come from the bathroom and he was watching it on his phone. At my friend's house, he was watching it on his phone and computer. How did I know he was watching it at their house? One of my friends called me in a nasty way. She was complaining about him watching porn and said he is welcome at her house, but his electronics are not welcome. He made her feel uncomfortable watching porn. Two months had passed and still no sex. I was so embarrassed and said he needed to calm down watching that shit everywhere, but I can't judge him; I had a sex addiction.

Some days I cried, begged, even took diet pills, would not eat but once a day, and was going to the gym. I was too afraid to eat food unless I was very hungry. Maybe I was too aggressive towards him, maybe I was too mean to him. I always tried to beg him to sleep with me; maybe I needed to back off of him. What am I doing wrong? Am I too big? Why is he with me? All these questions were going through my mind.

Could it be I'd been hard on him about my children, and making it clear for him to stay away from my children? I had to explain to him why I am like this. I told him I don't trust any man here on earth: not my dad, not my siblings, not even my children's dads. I am like this with everyone. I apologized, but this is a scar I could never get rid of. The shit hurts and still makes me emotional to this day.

I explained to him, also, I'd been molested many times, and why I like sex so much. "Please be patient with me, I've had to carry these scars and bags all my life. I never received counseling, just tough love. I had to learn to get over it on my own and pray to God to heal me. But I don't want that scar for my children or anyone's children to carry. If you need to watch porn, please watch it in our room and lock the door, or outside in your car."

I vented to so many friends and people. I needed help. I couldn't see clearly. Here it is, I am stressing over sex, and watching my husband's dick like a hawk. Why? What is wrong with me? God, please help me. I would be sitting in my car by myself, crying about my whole situation. Or sitting in the living room listening to those sad love songs. I'd been getting depressed, smoking a pack of cigarettes daily, and drinking a bottle of alcoholic beverage. Some days I was happy and next thing I know, I'd be crying so badly.

Thinking about all the shit I'd been through from my childhood years and up. Thinking about the days I needed my parents, and no one was there for me after being attacked. I wrapped my arms around me and curled up like a baby, crying. I didn't and still don't know why I used to get molested or raped. But I will kill a nigga dead if they touch my children. I also didn't know why people treated me like shit. I used to give people my heart and they ripped it away from me and ran with it, never to be seen anymore. If they did come back it was to see what else they could take.

I didn't want to see my children or anybody's children go through what I had gone through. I had to give my children tough love and teach them to speak their minds, because I didn't want the world to take advantage of them. I was giving them more responsibilities, especially my oldest. She had the most responsibility. I kept it real to my children about why their dads were not in their lives. I even gave the sex talk to my oldest daughter. I made sure I told her that a baby keep no man. I would say to her also, "Do you see any of your dads around?" She and my other children would say no. I said, "Do they take you to the doctors or school or do anything for you? All I get from your dads are child support, and that's all." I would tell them, "I don't want you to end up like me, but I want you to be better than me." I explained to them about heartbreak. That if someone breaks your heart, don't make yourself sick over them. To keep yourself busy, that when you are out of that person's sight, you are out of their mind. Best believe they moved on to the next person.

*****

Today is the start of my training. I am so nervous. I am going to be driving these big buses. I already took my CDL test a week ago. My instructor and I were driving in this big old lot for buses. I had to learn how to parallel park, k-turn, and back this bus up. I was okay on the bus, but when it came time for me to drive the stretchy bus with the rubber in the middle, it was so hard. I had a very hard time backing this bus up. It was like the back of the bus had a mind of its own. But I was excited; no more doing cashier.

They taught me how to operate and receive the fares on the bus, and how to do the paperwork.

At the end of my two weeks of training, I had to go out with another coworker to learn all the bus routes for the many different lines in my garage. Some of the men drivers did not care if I was on the bus with them on break time. One man just went to the back of the bus and took a piss. He explained to me that a lot of the lines don't have bathroom access, that there's going to come a time I may have to go.

Time passed by. I kept my schedule open, so that I could get calls to make my hours quickly. One line I was on had me so busy, I got off my bus looking for a bathroom. I couldn't find a bathroom, so I went to my coworker and asked her where do we go to the bathroom? She said I could use her cup as soon as she finished. I was so grossed out. I didn't want to use her cup. I was afraid her piss was going to splash on my bottom if I pissed in the cup. I was too afraid to piss at the back steps of my bus. So I walked back to my bus. I was going to hold my piss until the end of the trip. I had to piss really bad and I was only ten minutes from the end of my line. I tried to hold it, but the next thing I know, I pissed my pants. I was so embarrassed. My passengers saw liquid come from my seat onto the floor. One came up to me as he was exiting the bus and said, "It is unsanitary for me to be stepping in this stuff." I just gave him this evil look and rolled my eyes. I was so embarrassed; I didn't want to respond to him.

I had to call my office and tell them what happened. They told me to work to the end of the line and come straight to the garage. I was afraid for my coworkers to see or smell me. I hurried and tied my sweater around my waist. As soon as I gathered all my items off my bus, the maintenance man came to move the bus to clean it. All of a sudden, I heard the man yell "fuckkkkk" really loud. I was walking so fast in my office. One of my managers was watching me hard from the window to see if my clothes were wet. I stayed quiet and said nothing to anyone as I signed out. I drove straight home to wash my ass. This was the 2nd time I pissed myself. I won't pick this line ever again with no bathroom. After the second time that happened to me, I bought the big plastic cups, a box of gloves, and hand sanitizer. I was not going to let that happen to me no more.

I wore gloves every day driving the bus. Some of my passengers would be upset with me. But seeing where some of these people had their tickets, and after I caught ringworm on my face, never again would I touch those tickets without gloves. I never had ringworm a day in my life; it was so nasty, it was in the center of my right cheek on my face. Pus and crust were on it and very itchy. I had to get a prescription from my doctor. One night, a regular passenger got on my bus. He normally said hi to me, but this time he yelled out, "Yuck. What the fuck wrong with your face?" I was embarrassed because some of my passengers started looking.

Other bus lines were crazy. I had a man sneak on the back of my bus and he was being nasty to the other passengers. I had to make him get off my bus. I had some good passengers and some passengers who liked to give me problems. Some passengers were ready to fight me because I was doing my job and I would not let things slide. I needed my job. I was not trying to get fired or written up for no one. Some passengers were even bold enough to put their hands on me. I had to pop my brake on and get out of my seat to let them know I was not afraid of them. Some of the regular passengers would get on the people who'd be starting shit with me for no reason at all. Some of the passengers were upset about the bus fare. It was not my fault; I didn't make the fare. I just drive and collect the fare.

I made some friends also from driving the bus. I really liked my job and was having fun making money. I even made friends with this one female who was a passenger. I was getting this one line to New York and it seemed like I picked her up all the time. On her and my days off, I used to go by her house and pick her up. We then went to the park and played Frisbee or some kind of running games with my children. I even got to meet her wife; they were both really nice. I really enjoyed our friendship; she was like a little sister to me.

When I drove the bus, which was the last line to New York, I would tell her if I stop talking, talk to me because my ass was tired. It was hard staying up past 3:00 am. She would always bring me an energy drink and a snack when she got on my bus. I never asked her, she just did it out of the kindness of her heart. I didn't complain about the hours because I wanted to make fulltime and I had to do a lot of hours.

On the 3rd month, I was fulltime and had to pick a line. I was emotional because I was at the bottom of the list. I only had two people under me. The last three lines were to New York and all the lines were late. I had no choice but to pick one of the New York lines. The good thing about it was I had Tuesday and Wednesday off. At least on those days, I could take my children to doctors and do what I had to do on those days. I had to work from 4:00 pm until 1:45 am.

I met a lot of people driving the bus. Some of my coworkers were cool and would hang out on the bus with me.

*****

My marriage was a little rough. I was still begging for sex, but my hubby said he doesn't want to bother me. "Why don't you want to bother me?" I asked.

"Because you get off of work late, and you be looking tired," he said.

I said, "I don't care if I am dead tired, drooling in my sleep, this is your pussy. Get it whenever you want it. I will never say the word no to you. Sometimes sex is great, waking up to some good sex."

Still didn't work. Now I have been working for almost six months. My hubby and I had a conversation about moving out of my apartment.

I got in an argument with some nasty dog I slept with a while back before I knew my husband. That nasty jerk was disrespectful to my daughter. He said to my daughter, "I want to fuck you like I fucked your mother." My daughter was only 13 years old at the time. As soon as I got home from work, I went straight to the house to get my baseball bat.

"Where you going with that bat?" my husband asked.

"I will be right back," I said.

I rushed out to that man's house, banging and yelling at the man, Hak's, door. His grandmother opened the door.

I asked, "Where is Hak at?"

She said, "What's wrong?" I told her what he said to my daughter. She said, "Please don't call the cops."

"It ain't the cops he got to worry about, it's me he has to worry about."

She said, "He ain't home," and closed the door.

As soon as I got home, I asked my hubby not to send my daughter to the store by herself anymore. I told him what happened, and that's when he said we got to move. It was rough in my neighborhood, but everyone knew to mind their own business.

A week later, we started looking for apartments. I was so worried and afraid. *I can't afford the real-world rent if my husband decides to leave me.* But it was getting rough around my community.

We got a call back on a two-bathroom, three-bedroom house. The deal was, my hubby paid the rent and car insurance; I had to pay for everything else. I better make sure I keep my job, by any means necessary. I worked all the overtime I could get. I got new furniture, water bill, cable bill, new beds, etc. I liked that we no longer lived in the community we used to live. It felt somewhat safer for my children. The school was right around the corner, and so was the store. I never thought I'd be renting a house.

Between working and taking care of my family, I was busy. When I got home on this one day, my daughter said, "Mom, every time you leave out for work, Rudopho leaves out too." She said, "He doesn't come back until an hour before you get home."

Now, why is he coming home late? Maybe he was seeing that woman again, or someone new. So the next day was my day off. I got my daughter a cellular phone because there were no phones on in the house. Then I talked with my husband. I asked him why does he leave after I leave out for work? He walked away from me with no response. It was okay. I will remember this when I start to go out one day. I was not even upset. But my daughter was 16 years of age; she was old enough to watch her sisters and brothers.

Soon my friend's aunt found out that my kids were home alone. How? I don't know. She called me and said, "Why in the world are you leaving my babies home alone?"

"They're not alone. My oldest is watching them while I am at work."

Then she said, "That is too much responsibility for her to do every day." Especially that my work schedule kept rotating. She then said, "Don't leave my babies home no more. From now on when you have to work, bring my babies to my house. I will watch them for you until you get off of work."

"Thank you so much." I was relieved.

Every day when my kids got out of school, I drove my babies to my friend's Aunt Geraldine and gave her food and money to feed them. My children loved going to her house. I felt good. She truly treated me and my children like we were really her family. I was truly grateful for her help.

*****

I was off of work today, so I ran my errands, cleaned, cooked, and spent time with my children. Today was my husband's early day from work. I bought a bottle of wine and played my music after I got my children to bed. I love intimacy with some romantic music. Some of the words in those songs, and the voices you hear, it sounds like they are singing to me at that moment. Seems like it can make the sex great because it's like I am making love to the music.

Anyway, I tried to get some sex from my hubby, after I was talking to my dad about the situation. I always talk to my siblings or my mom and dad about sex. Sex was my whole life basically coming up. When you have a conversation with my family that's almost always one of our conversations. Or my family likes to joke with our mates whenever we would bring them around. Like some of the questions would be, "Are you spanking my daughter right?" and some other questions on that subject. We don't mean no harm, I guess it's in our genes.

For me, sex is a form of communication; I feel it is a bond between me and my mate. I love hard through sex; I love to touch my mate and I love to be touched by my mate sexually. To me, it is like my daily dose of medicine, it makes me happy and feel good for the moment. If it's darn good sex, I feel good for the whole day.

Anyway, my dad said some men like it when you undress them and so on. So, I used some of the pointers my daddy gave me. When my hubby got in the room, it was 8:00 pm and the kids were in the bed. We didn't have to work tomorrow. I unbuckled his pants. Because it's once again four months since we'd had sex.

"What are you doing?" he asked me.

"Just relax," I said. I got the buckle loose. Now I unbuttoned his pants.

He pushed me off of him so hard, I fell across the bed and hit my head on the dresser. I was so embarrassed and in pain. My ego went from 80 to 20. Never again will I try that again. I hurried up and put my clothes back on. I ran out of my house so quickly and rushed into my car. I could not help but wonder if he was still messing around on me. As soon as I got in my car, tears were running down my eyes. I was done with trying to make my marriage work.

I called the man my mom introduced me to a month ago. I needed to know what was wrong with me. I didn't know him very well; I would only run into him whenever I went to see my mom. Once in a blue, he would call me and we had a small conversation. I was trying to keep myself together while talking to him.

"Come pick me up," he said. He did not have to say it twice.

I drove to the front of my mom's place, and he was standing outside. The first thing he did was give me a hug as he got inside the car. Then the hug turned into a kiss, a long passionate kiss. This man was so fine, caramel-complexion, hair to his shoulders, nice body.

He said, "Let's get out of here."

"Okay," I said.

We ended up going to the hotel. He left out of the car and went to the front desk. Then he got back in the car and told me which room to go to. As soon as we got to the room, he came around and opened my door, grabbed me by the hand, then we went into the room.

I didn't tell him what happened. I was too embarrassed.

He turned on the shower and got naked in front of me. I was so excited, looking at his body. I guess he was excited too. I hoped I could handle it and him. He started taking my clothes off. I was so shy and nervous. Like I did not want him to look at my body. I felt like a fat blob. I was so afraid to let him see my body. But it was like he did not care about my weight. We both walked in the shower together. He made me feel like I was skinny. He washed me from neck to toe, rolls and all. Then he started washing, while I watched in a shy way. It was like I was in the shower with an exotic male dancer. I was too shy to move. I just stood there.

We then got out of the shower, and he dried me off. He started tongue kissing me, working his way down my neck to my back, down to my butt, then he turned me over and worked his way down to my breasts, then he eased me on the bed and worked his way down to my pleasure valley. It felt so good, but I felt so bad. I was married, but my husband wouldn't sleep with me. The way this man was kissing and sucking and touching me, my hubby never in his life touched me like this before. Kivi had me so wet and excited, he took all my stress away. Then he paused for a moment to get his condoms out of his wallet, magnum. I was ready. He kissed me some more in the valley, then he worked his way back up and slid himself inside of me. I was so excited, I couldn't keep quiet.

We used up the whole four hours having sex with one another. Then I took a shower and so did he. I dropped him off home, and I went home with a smile on my face.

My hubby asked me, "Where were you?"

"Out," I replied. I put on my pajamas and went to bed.

Ever since that night, Kivi and I talked on the phone almost every day. I was catching feelings for him. I didn't want to step outside of my marriage, but my hubby didn't want to sleep with me or spend much time with me. Our sex life stretched all the way to four months of no sex. He didn't want to sleep with me.

I started searching through my man's things and I found condom wrappers. Rudopho was home. I asked him, "Where did this condom wrapper come from?"

He started yelling at me. "What are you doing in my things?"

"I want to know why you are not sleeping with me."

He says he's tired, or sick.

"I should be the tired one. I do a lot: go to work, cook dinner, take care of my children, clean up the house, take the kids to school, but I still have time for sex with you."

We argued for almost an hour, then he asked me, "What do you want?"

"I want intimacy with you, and I want a baby."

We ended up having sex. I was to the point where I wanted to get pregnant now. I was getting older. I wanted one or two more babies before I turned 40.

*****

It's now our one-year anniversary and I saved up money to take my husband out since we didn't get to have a honeymoon. I made a reservation at this fancy restaurant that my coworkers were telling me about, reserved a hotel room with a heart-shaped jacuzzi in it, and the next day I was taking him to Atlantic City Casino. After I picked my children up from school, I went home to pack them an overnight bag, because they were going to my mother's home. I stopped at the store to get them some snacks, then I dropped them off. I went home to pick my hubby up because we were down to one car. His car broke down, so we shared his other car.

Before I could take him out, he had to stop in for a meeting. "Hurry," I said, "Our reservation is at 7:00 pm." It was already 6:00 pm.

I was upset because it was now 7:30. By the time he came out, it was 8:00 pm, so I just said we'd have to go to a chicken place and go. I didn't want him getting too tired and not wanting intimacy. I already had the wine and the music in my overnight bag. After getting the food, I drove to the hotel and checked in. My hubby and I went to the room. I set the candles around the jacuzzi and turned on the music. We ate and drank a little.

Then we got into the jacuzzi. He stayed in for ten minutes, then he got in the bed. I stayed in for another 25 minutes. I was enjoying the music and my drink. Then I got out of the jacuzzi and took a shower. Then I went into bed to get intimate with my hubby. He said, "Let me nap a little." Next thing I know it was already 2:00 am and we never had intimacy. So I went to sleep. We checked out the next day.

From there, we went to Atlantic City to go to the casino and have lunch. I said it was his turn to treat me since we didn't have sex last night.

"Okay," he said.

"I will never celebrate our anniversary ever again," I told him.

"That's fine," he said.

I was disappointed that everything didn't go as planned, but I learned not to do anything nice for him no more. Like on Father's Day, I took him out to dinner and got him some gifts. For Mother's Day, I got a plant. His birthday, I took him out; my birthday, I got a cake and some women's panties. I'm done being nice. I will treat him like he treats me.

As soon as we left the casino, we went straight to my mom's to get my children and went home. I will never celebrate another anniversary ever again.

*****

My car broke down and I needed to hurry to work. The cab said it would be an hour before anyone could get to me. I was getting nervous. So, I called one of my coworkers, Rob. I explained my situation to him. He said he'd be there in five minutes. Thank God. I stayed outside waiting for him. I was anxious to get to work. I did not want to get written up for a late show-up. As soon as Rob came, I jumped straight in his car after kissing Rudopho and my children. He got me to work really fast. I was so relieved. I had ten minutes to spare. I got all my paperwork together and ran to get my bus. I was a little behind schedule due to the work rush hour traffic. Other than that, the day went by pretty fast.

My day was now finished and I wanted to hurry home to play the lottery. The jackpot was really high. So, I asked a couple of coworkers for a ride. This older man gave me a ride home. He was flirting with me, but I didn't respond back. I offered him gas money. I just smiled as he flirted and reminded him that I am married. As soon as he got close to my house, I asked him nicely to drop me off at the corner store. I thanked him and jumped out of the car.

I only had 20 minutes left to play my lottery. I got in line, then when it came to my turn, I was telling the man the numbers. He made me get out of line and fill out a slip. As soon as I filled out the slip, I got in line and the man played the numbers. I paid him and then picked up some snacks for my children.

When I opened the store door and stepped on the sidewalk, a car came speeding on the sidewalk and almost hit me. The man yelled at me and asked if I was just on Aldine Street.

"What? Nigga, I just got off work. You see me in my uniform?"

He got out of the car and said, "Nah, you were just on my street."

I was worried now because I'd never seen this man before. So, I went back to the store and called the police. The man followed me inside. I told the man I didn't know what was going on and I'd never seen him before. I yelled, "Ask the store. Matter of fact, look at their camera. I have been in this store for almost a half-hour."

I saw the man had a gun on his hip, so I was not leaving until the police got there.

Next thing I know, some woman came in the store with a little boy. The woman said to her son, "Do you see her?"

Me and the store owner were looking at her like, "What are they talking about?" while I was waiting for the police.

The boy yelled, "No, Mom, the person's not here."

Then the mother said to her son, "The bitch is right here."

"Excuse me, what is going on? I am not a bitch."

She said, "You were in my fucking house."

"What! Bitch, I just got off of work." I didn't know if they were trying to rob me. I had my paycheck in my pocket, which was a little over $900.00. I said to the woman, "I just got off of work and got dropped off at the store. You have a case of mistaken identity."

She said she and her hubby will be outside waiting.

I said, "Okay, good because the police are on their way."

As soon as the police came, the people were long gone. So, the officer gave me a ride home. He told me to call him if I had any more problems. I don't know what that shit was about, but I was worried. Now I know how people feel with mistaken identity.

I told Rudopho what happened. I also said we all are going to church on Sunday before I go to work. He replied okay.

Sunday morning, I cooked breakfast, washed myself up, and ironed my babies' clothes for church. My children were not babies, but I had a habit of calling them my babies. My children ate their breakfast and got dressed. I grabbed my Bible and we all got in the car for church. As soon as I got to the church, it was like the Word was for me. I was emotional and crying like a baby. I happened to lift my head up and look to the left. The man was smiling at me. I stopped crying and had a serious expression on my face.

I said to Rudopho, "That's the guy that tried to hit me with his car."

Next thing I know, I saw his wife and the little boy from the store. So, he looked and said okay.

After service was over, I saw she was talking to the pastor who was also my pastor at the new church I went to from time to time.

In a nice, normal tone, I asked the woman, "Did you find the real person who came to your house?"

She said, "Yeah, it was you."

I said to the woman, "It was not me. I promise you it was not me."

She said it was, so then I told the pastor the situation.

"Bitch, I'm going to fuck you up in the parking lot," she yelled to me.

The pastor looked at her and tried to talk to her. I said it was not me and started leaving the church. I had to be to work in two hours and I wanted to cook dinner before I left.

Next thing I know, my children, Rudopho and I were walking to the car, and I heard, "Bitch, I'm going to kick your ass."

I kicked off my high heels and got ready to fight. I was really upset. Me and this woman and her husband were arm's-length close to one another. All of a sudden, I was blocked by Rudopho. I was yelling at him to get off of me. I was trying to get at that woman to fight her. She really had some nerve, accusing me, and now she was bold enough to come to my car. Rudopho would not let me go. Next thing, I see my daughter was about to fight the woman. Everyone in that parking lot came and separated the woman from my daughter.

I was very angry and embarrassed that I acted a fool in the parking lot. I was trying to tell the woman it was not me. The church people told me to leave and the pastor gave me the woman's last name.

I went straight to the police department and explained the whole situation to them. They sent someone to the woman's house. He didn't tell me where she lives, but an officer came to my home and said they spoke to the woman. They said she apologized and she realized that I did not go to her house. I said, "Yes, I've never seen them a day in my life until her husband tried to hit me with his car." Since that day, I've never seen nor heard from those people again. I had to apologize to the church people. I did not mean to disrespect them.

But I was arguing with Rudopho for grabbing me. "What if those people would have hit me, and you grabbing me?" The situation could have gotten really bad, but thank God, it didn't get out of hand.

*****

After living at the new place for two years, some man said we had to move. He said the house was in foreclosure and if we don't move, the city will evict us in a month. I asked, "How? We just paid rent to the landlord." The man said he owes a lot of money and showed us the paperwork. So, we started looking for a new place to move. We ended up moving three weeks later to Tremont.

Then my hubby said he had to go away for eight months on a business trip. I was very emotional. I really tried to be intimate with him. He kept pushing me away, but he was still carrying condoms in his wallet. I didn't say anything to him about it. I didn't want to argue anymore, I just wanted more time with him. It was now six months without sex and he was leaving me for eight months.

When he left, my cousin came to help me for a month. My cousin was a great help. I worked while she took care of my babies. When it was time to go to the grocery store once a week, I let her help me pick out the groceries. I vented to her about my marriage.

"You need to leave him. You're a pretty woman. If I was you, I would stop sleeping with him unprotected. You don't know what he will bring back home to you," she said. "Matter of fact, he wants to stay with you, just stay with him. This is the longest you've been in a relationship. Just do what you got to do to make you happy," she also said to me.

You know what? Almost all of my friends told me to do the same thing. When we left the store, I started thinking about what she and some of my friends had told me.

My cousin would take my children to many different places and read books to them at night like I used to do before working overnight at my job. I was glad she kept my routine; my children loved bedtime stories. That month went by fast, and then I had better work hours. I was able to be home in the daytime with my children and work at night.

It was hard doing everything on my salary: the electric bill was $900.00 a month, plus buying food, and all the other bills. My husband mailed me the rent money and he paid the car insurance online. I paid for everything else. But the area I lived in was rough;

there was always a fight in front of my home and I lived on the first floor of a three-family house. The landlord lived on the 2nd floor. Our bill was too high, but he would never let the electric company come to read the meter. He wrote our numbers on a piece of paper and gave it to the meter man from the electric company. He was a nice landlord, but something seemed fishy about the electric bill. He worked for a candy company and always brought candy to me for my children.

I used to complain to him about my heat bill, and question why he didn't let the power company in. He never would give me a clear answer. His way of helping me with the electric bill was putting a lockbox on my thermostat.

"Why would you do something like that? That's not going to help me with my electric bill."

The landlord replied he will set it on one temperature to help me save on my bill. Then he put the key in his pocket and left my house.

I said, "Hold up. I should have that key to set the temperature on whatever I like since I have to pay the bill."

He sat there and thought about it, and then he still left with the key. This was horrible. I wanted to move out of this place. I was paying a $1000.00 rent for a three-bedroom and $900.00 for electricity. So not worth my money.

*****

One day I was putting the clothes in the car, so we could go to the laundromat. Then some men with long coats started walking in my house, yelling.

"Ma, Mommy," my kids said.

I turned around and asked the two men, "Why are you in my house?"

They were detectives and looking for someone from the fight.

"Well, you are at the wrong house," I said. He asked me if I knew the people. "No, I do not," I replied.

Then he left me his business card and the two men left. After they left and I finished putting the clothes in the car, I went and got my children. I was not going to let my children sit and wait in the car, because a lot of cars used to speed on my street. A car slammed into my van the night before and smashed the passenger side sliding door in. I was ready to move. Too much action on my block. I was complaining to Rudopho so much. He would call me once every night before he went to bed.

As soon as Rudopho came home from his business trip and rested for the day, I tried the next day to be intimate. No luck yet. I kept trying because I was getting up in age. I wanted another baby so badly. I missed holding a baby and the feeling of being pregnant. My children were bigger. They would not even let me kiss them on their cheek anymore when I dropped them off to school. After being home for one month, Rudopho said he had to leave for another eight months. I was really emotional and bothered. It hurt me so.

"You just got home. You will only be home for six months." Since he'd come home, we took my children to a couple different amusement parks, museums, movies, and had small cookouts at the park. I wanted to keep my babies busy. I was feeling guilty because I was working so much and didn't get to spend much time with my babies. My work schedule was so horrible. But I needed the money to support my family.

Some days, my hubby and I went to look for a new location to move. We'd been house hunting for a couple of months. Anyway, we stopped looking in Newark and started looking for a new place to move in Irvington, NJ. We found a five-bedroom home in Irvington with a basement. This house was old but really big. I liked the house a lot, and the location. We had a large front porch, living room, and kitchen. This house had three floors. The bedrooms where my children slept were on the 2nd floor, and the 3rd floor, which was the attic, was huge also, and it had another room on the side of it. The house was a little creepy. Some of the doors had skeleton keys; the dining-room door was a sliding door you could lock with the skeleton key. It could use some fresh paint on the walls, and the landlord gave me permission to paint with light colors. The landlord said he did not want us to have access to the basement. I asked him why, when we were paying $1500.00 for rent. He said because he had his things in the basement and he didn't want anyone in the basement.

After being in that house for a month, I invited my kids' godmother over. We were talking about my marriage situation. I was crying about my marriage to her. I even opened up about the one time my hubby came home; how if I was off of work, I would greet him by the door with a hug and a kiss. Well this particular day, he came home early from work. I walked up to kiss and hug him, but he pushed me and ran upstairs. I then heard the shower water running.

Later that night I asked him, "Why did you have to take a shower?" He replied he was dirty. I said, "You sure looked clean to me."

I was sitting, thinking the worst. Who was he seeing?

Because the week before, some woman at the bar came running up to him, about to hug and kiss him. He blocked her very quickly and said, "This is my wife."

Her eyes got big. "Oh, hello, nice to meet you," she said, and she walked away.

I was thinking, "What was that about?" Why did she give me that look and walk away?

I always vented to her as well as some of my other friends. I know they were tired of hearing me complain. Sometimes I'd be thinking: "I am stressing too much, or feel as if I am doing something wrong in my marriage." Then I was stressing about how I didn't have much time with my children. I had to do my best to support my children, by working overtime. I even complained about wanting to be pregnant; I wanted another baby so badly.

I set up an appointment and got tested to see if I was still fertile. They said I was still fertile, that Rudopho needed to come in to get tested. But he refused to get tested. The test was so expensive. I hated that I spent that much money for the test.

My kids' godmother listened to me for a while and gave me her advice. Then she said next Saturday she wanted to host a party at my house. "I work for this new company," she said. "So, invite your other friends and tell everyone to bring some money. I want to teach you how to take care of yourself."

I said, "I do take care of myself. What is it you are trying to sell me?"

"You will see next week," she responded. Then she got up, gave me and the kids a hug, and then she left.

The next day, I went to work. I got a phone call from my oldest daughter. She was crying and worried. She said my twins were fighting, and my son pushed my daughter down the stairs. She then came upstairs and whacked him in the head with her hard doll head.

She said the blood was squirting out of his head and he was running around screaming and crying. I told her to hurry and get a rag and press it on his forehead for five minutes. I was talking to her through my wireless headphones while I was working. I was so scared and worried. I stayed on the phone with her. After five minutes, I told her to take off the rag.

She said, "It's not bleeding no more."

"Good, now make all of them go in your room and watch television. Did everyone eat dinner?" I asked.

My daughter responded, "Yes."

"Good, don't let them out until I get home. The only time they leave out is to go to the bathroom."

I didn't get off of work until 11:00 pm that night.

Another time I was at work, my son was playing swords with the curtain rod. He made a mistake and stepped back on the curtain rod. As soon as I got off of work, he showed me his feet, and I took him straight to the emergency room. His feet were not bleeding, but I took him just in case he needed stitches.

He said, "Mom, it doesn't hurt."

I wrapped his foot with a bath towel. I asked, "Why didn't you tell your sister to call me?"

He replied, "She said to squeeze it with a towel."

When the emergency room called us in the back, they said they had to give him some stitches. He cried while they gave him some numbing medicine in his feet. Once his feet were numb, they started stitching. They sent us home with a prescription and instructions on how to care for his feet. He had to stay home for five days. So, the next day I turned in the paperwork requesting five days off. I was happy to be home, so I could spend more time with my babies. We didn't go anywhere special, because he couldn't put on his shoes. So, we stayed home and worked on homework and arts and crafts, plus read books. I was also glad to have been home.

One day I was going out of the side door to take out the trash. I saw a man coming in with a key. I was afraid and asked him who he was and what he was doing here. He responded that he lives there in the basement.

"How long have you been living here in the basement?" I asked.

His name was Alex and he said he had been living there for a couple of years. Wow, really? That's why Mr. Anderson the landlord didn't want us to use the basement. I called Mr. Anderson, and his wife answered the phone. I asked her why they didn't tell me someone lives in the basement. She said he just moved in.

I said, "No, he lived there for two years. Are you taking something off of our rent?" She said no, because he was not using our electric bill. "Okay, I will remember that," I told her.

Later that day, I heard a key coming in my front door. I knew it was not my husband; he was at work. My children were at school and my son was asleep. I was ass naked, running downstairs to the laundry room to get me a clean towel. As soon as I got to the bottom of the stairs, Mr. Alexander walked straight into the house.

"What the fuck is your problem? Why the fuck are you in my house? Get out of here!" I yelled at him.

I hurried and ran to get the towel, and I heard him say "nice."

I was so upset; this jerk was still standing there. He said he had to fix the kitchen sink plumbing.

I asked him, "Aren't you supposed to call me first?" He said no, it's his house and he owns it. I said, "Yeah, but I am renting it. Now get out of my house. Next time you need to call me."

I was really upset and called my hubby. All he said was okay.

This jerk still didn't leave and he went in the kitchen to fix the plumbing. So, I called his wife, because she was black; her husband was not. To my understanding, black women don't like it when their man is seeing another woman.

As soon as his wife Ebony picked up the phone, I said, "Hi Ebony, this is your tenant."

She responded, "I know who you are."

"Okay, well, I just want you to know that I was walking around downstairs butt naked, nothing on, and your husband came in my house."

She yelled, "What?"

I said, "Yeah, he stuck his key in my front door and came into the house with no warning and he's still in my house. He refuses to leave and said it's his house. He also said 'nice' to me when he seen me naked."

She said, "Let me call you back." Next thing I know, she called him and he left my house.

Later that night, she came and apologized to me. I showed her in the lease that as long as we are tenants, they can't be walking into the house. She said she promised he won't do that anymore. After she left, me and my children were talking. I told them if anyone came in the house while I was at work to call me as soon as possible.

I also said to my oldest daughter, "Don't let no one in while I am at work."

She responded, "Okay."

After that, I listened to my children crack jokes on one another. Two of my children were so funny with the things they were saying; I don't know where they get this mess from. I am dingy and silly, but not funny.

During my five days off from work, on the days my other children had to go to school, I had to wrap my son's feet up and help him to the car. On the last night that I was off work, we had junk food night and a movie. We started having junk food night every Friday or Saturday night with a movie in the DVD player.

My children were fighting a lot as they got older; they were so spoiled. My oldest and second oldest were fighting the most, even when they were being watched by my cousin. She told me when they fought, she sprayed water on them from her water bottle and placed them in time out. But if other people tried to fight them, they all stuck together and protected each other.

Some of my family would straight out say my kids were spoiled and rotten. I replied, "No they are not."

Then I would have my children question, "Mom, why don't we get to see our other family?"

I always said, "I am always busy."

I didn't really see family too much except some of my sisters and my brother, and my mom and cousin. I got tired of hearing my family talking crap about me having too many kids. Or some of them said I cannot come to their house with all my children. But when my family came to my house, or even my friends, when I feed my kids, I feed everyone who is in my home. I treat everyone's kids like my children.

*****

My brother called me and said he was moving back to New Jersey. I said, "Okay, that's great." I missed my baby brother so much.

He said, "Guess where I am moving?"

"Where?" I responded.

"With you. big sis."

"Okay, come on. I'd love to have you over. Good, you can help your niece watch your other nieces and nephews."

"No problem, big sis."

I was so excited he was moving in. I told Rudopho. He responded that it was not a problem. He was glad to have him live with us since Rudopho had to travel again. My children loved their uncle so much.

*****

Some days after work, I invited some of my female coworkers over with their kids, and said, "Those who can bring a dish, bring something, or if you can't bring something, still come and eat." I supplied the bottles of wine and food when they would come over. I let their children run through the house or outside with my children, and us woman would sit and enjoy the music and we'd talk about almost everything.

One day I was having a cookout and invited some people over. While I was cooking and setting the tables up outside, the power went off in the house. Next thing I know, the man in the basement came outside and asked me if my power was off. I responded yes. I asked him the same question and he said yes. So, I called my landlord's wife Ebony. I was upset now.

I said to her, "I thought your husband's cousin had his own electric bill."

She said, "He do."

I yelled, "All lies."

She said, "He has his own power bill," again then started arguing.

I told her I was calling the police, and that I'd found out he's not supposed to be living in the basement from my old real estate agent. She apologized to me. I also told her I found out he was using my electric bill. I told her when my power went out, his power went out also. The electric company came and shut the power off for non-payment. I paid my bill, but whatever she did, it screwed our account up. So I called the electric company. Come to find out, she set the account up for us to pay her old bill. I was so angry about the whole situation. I wished I'd never moved into this house. I had to rush out of the house and go to the electric company with my receipts.

The woman at the electric company looked at the money I'd been paying and saw that we were not late on our payments. She said our landlord, Ebony, had the bill going to her past bill and not my bill. So, the lady at the electric company straightened everything out. She also said an emergency technician would be at my house within one hour. I also found out from her we had one meter, and that the man in the basement was using my electric for the past couple of months.

I then called Ebony and told her that I found out what she had done and that her husband's cousin was on my electric. I told her to refund me my money and lower my rent. Ebony responded that she would be there to talk with me later. I hurried home to finish cooking and setting up for the cookout.

I liked it when I could entertain people. I didn't have much to offer, but whatever I had, I shared it. Once in a blue, I would travel to my one friend's house, but her ass was stingy as heck. I always had to feed my children at home or wait until she was feeding her children, and then me and my kids would go out to eat. But let me do what she does—not feed her kids when I feed mine—and she would be so upset. I don't understand her sometimes, but I stay in touch with her only because we grew up together. I could never understand her nasty attitude, though. I am glad I'm not a jerk like her.

Later that day, after my cookout had ended and everyone left, Ebony the wife of the landlord came to my house. She said she can give me 25 dollars a month for him using just our lights. She said he didn't have anything electric in his house.

I said to Ebony, "Why are you lying to me? He has a stove, a washer, and a dryer, a microwave, and he's using my water."

Ebony's eyes got so big and she looked like she was angry.

141

"You got to give me more than that and go down on my rent."

She then said she can lower my rent to $1300.00 and give me $125.00 a month for electricity.

"Okay, thank you. Now, are you also going to give me a refund for the exterminator I had to hire? That man in the basement is nasty. He doesn't take his trash out and I have roaches. I didn't have roaches when I moved into this place."

She said no, she's not going to refund me for the exterminator, but she will continue to pay for the exterminator to come once every month.

I liked the house, but I didn't like my shady landlords. One day Alex the landlord came to the house while I was at work. My daughter called and said he just came in the house. I told her to put the phone on speaker.

I then said to Alex if his ass doesn't get out of my house, that I will call the police on his ass.

He left, then he called me on my phone and said he cut the water off to my house.

I responded, "Why would you do some mess like that? You do know I have a lot of children and when they have to use the bathroom, they are still going to use it. So go ahead and shut the water off. The problem is going to be worse, especially if they have to take a shit. You are going to have a lot of mess to clean up."

Alex did not like what I said and he turned the water back on. I told Alex he needed to give me a couple of days' notice to make sure that I am home. When no one's home, he is not allowed in my home with my children. He agreed to give me notice for the next time he had to work on something in the house.

*****

I am so happy my brother moved in with us today. I did not have to pick him up from the bus station. He caught the taxi to my house, being I was at work. I left him a key with my oldest daughter. When I got off of work, I stayed up and chatted with my brother for a while, then I went to bed so I could be ready for work in the morning. My brother was becoming a big help. He used to cook dinner and help my children keep the house clean.

Before I got home from work on my payday, I would buy two bottles of alcoholic beverages and hide it in my room. I like to have drinks on the nights my friends come over. One day I went to get my liquor from my secret stash for my company. I only had two bottles left. I should have had eight bottles! I said something to Rudopho and he said he and my brother had been drinking them. He thought I bought it for the house. I was so upset and told him it was not for them to drink. That was for my company. After those two bottles were used for my company, I did not buy any more beverages until it was on the day I planned to entertain my company.

During working that week, I had made friends with some male who was a detective. I met him at the grocery store. We talked on the phone for a couple of days. He invited me out for a drink three days after meeting him. I accepted his invitation. I met him at the bar and we sat there having a nice conversation. I blushed at some of the things he was saying to me. I had my head down, looking at my drink, slowly sipping on it. It was a sweet alcoholic beverage. I had half a glass left of my drink.

I happened to look up and I saw this guy looking at me. I looked at the man who was smiling at me; he was an old classmate named Zinc.

I said, "Zinc." He said my name. Then we got out of our seats and gave each other a hug. We chatted for five minutes and exchanged phone numbers. I wanted to leave with Zinc, he was looking so good. We were flirting with one another.

My date, David, had this serious look on his face. I went to the bathroom after talking to Zinc. When I came out, my friend David said to me, "Who was that?"

I told him, "My old classmate." I didn't tell him he was flirting with me. David asked me if I was ready to go. I responded, "Yes, I am ready."

He kept insisting that I finish my drink. I didn't want to finish my drink, because I went to the bathroom. He asked me for a 4th time to finish my 2nd drink because he doesn't like to waste money, so I said okay and picked up my drink and finished it. He got into his car and I followed him in my car. He invited me back to his place. He only lived five minutes from the bar. As soon as I got to his house, I was feeling really nice, and then dizzy.

I woke up the next morning, not remembering what happened last night. I know I was naked and the sheet was off of his bed. I asked him what we did last night, and he responded, "We had sex."

I asked, "How did we have sex and I don't remember? Did we at least use a condom?"

He said yes and he said he had to stop because I threw up on me and him. He said I was so drunk and sex was good. I don't understand how I was so drunk when I only had two drinks. As I was getting dressed, I saw dried up vomit all over his floor on the side of the bed.

I hurried and left his house. I was upset. I texted and asked him if he put something into my drink. He replied no. How did I pass out only having two drinks? I left his butt alone. I didn't trust him anymore. That was sneaky what he did.

How was I ever going to explain to my husband where I was? I didn't mean to spend the night out. This is crazy!

I looked through my phone. I saw my hubby called me a lot of times. I had to wait out a while to make sure Rudopho was at work. As soon as I got home, I showered and cooked my children breakfast. I was thinking about what happened the night before, how I broke my own rule, never to drink a drink I left at the bar. I didn't tell anyone about what happened to me; I just kept it to myself. The situation made me very embarrassed.

*****

Today is the day my friend is coming over. I started cleaning and mopping the floors in the house, while my hubby was watching television in our bedroom. The children were either playing on their video games or watching television. My brother was at work; he started a new job a couple of days ago. He worked days and I worked evenings and nights.

I wanted to make sure the house was fresh and clean, so I went upstairs to mop my room floor and the stairs attached to my room. As soon as I mopped the 3rd step, I fell down the stairs along with the bucket. My hubby Rudopho got up and asked what happened.

Still, on the floor, I replied, "I fell."

He said, "Oh," and went back into the room to watch television.

I couldn't believe this asshole did not try to help me up. I just got up and finished cleaning. I had a little time before Sinka came over to sell some stuff. I couldn't wait to see what it is. I only got eight people to come over. The others didn't want to come, because they didn't know what it was my friend Sinka was selling. As soon as 8:00 pm came, Sinka rang the doorbell. I let her in. She was carrying a huge duffle bag. She told us all to have a seat. We all sat there waiting, wanting to know what was in the bag.

She started talking and setting up the table I cleaned off. She pulled out this white item with a purple head.

"What is that?" I asked.

"A vibrator," she said. "For the g-spot."

"What?" I never used toys before. I think it's nasty to touch yourself. I tried with my fingers as they do in the movies, but I felt nothing, so I stopped.

Anyways, while she was explaining how each toy is to be used, it piqued my curiosity. I wanted to buy some of these toys. My friends and I bought some stuff. Me, I bought the lube, the g-spot, and the bullet, which looked like a small egg, and a dildo.

After she and my other friends left, I went upstairs and took a shower. Then I asked my husband if he'd like to try the toys with me. He said, "No, but I will watch."

I tried the g-spot first. Nothing. No excitement yet, after moving the toy around trying to find a spot. Then I stopped and I lubed my clitoris up and tried the little one shaped like an egg. It had seven speeds on it. I put it on the max speed. I liked how it felt in my hand. I touched it lightly on my clitoris. After moving it around, I started getting very excited. I started feeling my vagina vibrating and my hand was shaking. Next thing you know, my legs started trembling. I felt warm stuff coming out. I felt like I peed the bed, my whole butt was wet.

My hubby was smiling, saying, "You had an orgasm."

Wow, is that what that was? I'd never experienced a feeling like this before. Why can't this happen when I am having sex? This felt so good. I started using this toy almost every night, three times or more. This time I placed two towels under my butt. It sure took my daily stress away. I was using the toy so much, it was giving me stomach cramps. I liked these toys, but I had to learn to stop after my second orgasm.

Sometimes I was using these toys, and when my hubby came in, he would join in. I played with the toys purposely to get my husband to join in. As soon as I got him to join, I'd put my toys down, then he would say, "Pick your toy back up." Last time I let him play with me with my toys he was kind of rough. That shit did not feel good. But I did not want to mess up his involvement with my toys and me.

Another night, I wanted sex from my hubby without the toys. He just came in from a night out with his friends. It was midnight. I asked him for some, and he made up some excuse. I asked, "Why are you saving yourself to go jerk off somewhere?" That started an argument. Next thing I know, we were having sex.

All of a sudden, I started smelling a different aroma. All the years I'd been with him, I never smelled a smell like this. He smelled like he was fucking already. "Get off of me you nasty dog."

I ran straight in the bathroom and jumped in the shower with a bottle of vinegar and water douche. I came back into the room and said, "Next time, shower before you ever touch me."

I was so upset, I just went to bed. It was not even worth my time to argue with him. I won't argue about sex anymore. I am good. If he doesn't want to sleep with me, it's okay. I am going to do my best to keep his name out of my mouth, out of my conversation. I am just going to be his sexless wife since that's what he wants. But I won't be sexless. He doesn't want to leave me, and I don't want to leave him. I will find other ways to please myself.

I was even getting upset that I wasn't pregnant yet. What's the problem? I'd never had a hard time having a baby. I need to have a baby soon. I'm getting older. I wanted to have two more children before I get in my 40s.

*****

My sister called me and said they were coming up for the weekend. She said she wanted us to go out. She said I needed to get out for the weekend and she was not going to let me say no. She always tried to get me to go out at least once or twice a year. I almost always made excuses.

Anyway, as soon as my sister came to New Jersey, we went out the next night. We dropped my children off to my mom's house. From there, she drove me and my other sister to some bar. Since she doesn't drink, I was heavily drinking with my other sister. It was like we were trying to out-drink one another.

I was talking about everything I'd gone through, past and present. I was crying about us not being so close. I was even upset that I was the fat one and the ugly one. How I had to grow up the way I did, and how we did not get the chance to grow up together. I was a mess, and the drinks were not making me feel any better.

My sister stopped me and said, "You need help. You need counseling."

She was right. Maybe I do need counseling; I know people are tired of me venting to them. I was getting sick and tired of me complaining to everyone. I was sounding like a broken record. I tried to stay quiet, but it hurt so bad with the shit I'd been through from my past.

We left that bar and went to another bar. This time, they would not let me talk. I guess I embarrassed them at the last place. When we got to this new place, my sister pulled me to the dance floor, and we started dancing. Then men started dancing with us, and I started having fun. The music was nice, the lights dim.

I still had some more drinks. We stayed out until 6:00 am. I was so tired when my sisters dropped me off at home.

I was in bed until noon the next morning. I woke up with a nasty headache. Never again will I drink like that. I was trying to keep up with my baby sister. I remember last time I was so drunk, I got my ass in the bed, it felt as if my bed was spinning around. I don't like that feeling.

*****

I only had one week to be with Rudopho before he leaves me again. This time I am dropping him off at the airport. I called out of work on the day he had to go. I dropped my children off to my mom and we went to the hotel. When we were at the hotel, I was an emotional mess in front of him. I was crying like a little kid, snot running out of my nose and everything. I tried to be intimate with him, but my period was on.

Then my job called me and said, "After you drop your hubby off today, come straight to work or you will be suspended. We don't have no one to cover your schedule," she said. I was really upset now. So once I dropped my hubby off to the airport, I went straight to work.

I went out to do my bus route to Bloomfield, NJ. Then one of my regular passengers said to me, "Why are you not smiling?" I ignored her. Then she said, "Hey, bus driver, why are you not smiling?"

I replied, "I am not having a good day," and I kept driving the bus.

When I got to her bus stop, she wrote her phone number on a paper. Then she said, "Call me if you want to hang out sometimes," then she asked for my number. I didn't think much about it. I gave her my phone number. Then she got off my bus, and I continued with my work.

A couple of days passed and I was busy, between taking care of my children and working. I had a lot of errands to run today. After I took my children to school, I headed to the grocery store. Then my phone rang.

"Hello? Who's calling?"

"Val."

"Val who?"

"The lady you met on your bus."

"Okay, I remember you."

"I was just checking on you to see how you are doing," Val responded.

"I been okay, just missing my hubby, that's all."

"We need to hang out, or go to lunch so you can get your mind off your husband," Val responded. "When is your next day off of work?"

"I will be off on Thursday, which is a couple of days from now."

"Okay, cool. We can meet for lunch," she said.

"Sure, what time and where?"

"If you pick me up, I can show you how to get to this nice restaurant in Kearny," Val responded.

"Sure, not a problem. See you soon." Then we hung up.

After I finished my shopping and checked out, I went to a couple of places to pay some bills. Then I headed home so I could put up the groceries and clean up the house. I got a phone call from one of my friends. She wanted to know if my daughter and I could babysit her kids on my days off. I said, "Sure, no problem." She used to let me use her car sometimes when my car would break down, so I didn't mind watching her babies. I loved her kids like my own. All five of her kids would call me Auntie T. I used to

159

watch them from time to time. They would never want to go home.

The days surely go by fast when you have a lot to do. I was busy every day: working, cleaning, doctor visits, spending time with my children, and taking them to different places, and now babysitting. Well, my daughter was getting paid $25.00 to watch her kids, even though I was the one really watching them.

My friend Estel was only supposed to bring her kids to my house on my days off. But her slick ass waited until I went to work and dropped her kids off at my house. My cousin was at my home calling me. I couldn't answer the phone until I was at the end of my line. I broke my headphones by mistake.

As soon as I called her, she said, "Do you know whose kids are these at your house?"

"What?"

"It's five little kids at your house and the car drove off."

I was upset because Estel did not call me to tell me she was dropping her kids off. We agreed to my days off. My daughter was at work.

My cousin said, "I am not watching no extra kids." She was fussing on the phone. "Tell her to come get her kids."

I hung up with my cousin and called Estel. She would not answer her phone. I called my cousin and asked her to just watch them today and I'd pay her extra. I continued working my line, and once my work was complete, I hurried home.

My cousin said, "I didn't mean to be so fussy. I didn't know what was going on. I opened the door and all these kids come running in and the car sped off. Your kids said that's their cousins."

"Yeah, they fake cousins," I replied. "I will have a talk with Estel as soon as she gets off of work."

Then my cousin got her things and left the house.

It is now 1:00 am. Estel got off of work at 10:30. I started calling her phone, but no answer. I fussed her answering machine out. That was my fourth time calling her and no response. Then my doorbell rang at 1:30 am. She came in with a fake stink attitude. She had the nerve to ask me why I was calling her phone so much.

"You never said I had to babysit today when you know me and my daughter work today."

She was saying, "Okay, okay," in a rude way. Then she grabbed her kids and left. She was sitting in her car for a while. "My baby pissy," she yelled to me from her car. "No one didn't change his diaper."

I replied, "I changed his diaper as soon as I got in from work. You need to stop buying those cheap three-dollar diapers. If a baby pisses in it one time, the diaper is finished."

Next thing I know, she changed his diaper and got back in the front seat. Before she drove off, this nasty bitch threw the diaper in front of my door. "It's okay, I'll see you at work tomorrow."

She was upset because my daughter and I weren't watching those kids anymore. I was done with her ass. She was lucky I was too tired to get in my car and go slap her in the face with that diaper. She always tried to take advantage of me. I am so done with Estel.

*****

It was now Thursday, and I got a call from Val. She asked me if I was on my way. I looked at the time. It was 11:30 am. I overslept. I had to hurry to wash my children up and get them to school. I was exhausted from the double I did at work the night before, I didn't get home until 2:00 am.

"I will be a little late, but I am on my way."

"Okay, see you soon," Val replied.

After I got washed and dressed, I got my children off to school. I headed straight to Val's house.

As soon as I got to her house, she got in my car, and she was showing me how to get to the restaurant in Kearny. We had small conversations on our way to the restaurant. When we got there and sat at a table, I ordered breakfast, and she ordered herself lunch.

I was sitting, talking about my marriage. I sounded like a broken record. But I really missed my husband. She didn't complain, she just listened. After eating, we stopped by the store, and then I was headed to her house. As soon as we got in front of her door, she started talking to me. She was telling me about herself and her job. I had to interrupt her.

"Sorry Val, we have to cut this conversation short. I have to go."

"What is wrong?" Val asked me.

"I got to piss."

"You can use my bathroom," Val said.

"It's okay, I can go somewhere, to the store."

"Why are you going to find a bathroom, when you can use my bathroom?" replied Val.

"Okay, I will use your bathroom. I really have to go." I was doing the peepee dance into her house, trying not to go on myself. After I used the bathroom, I washed my hands. I opened the bathroom door and she was right there.

"What's wrong with you?" I asked.

She said nothing and went straight for my neck. The way she sucked on my neck and rubbed my breast at the same time, I didn't think anything of it. I got excited, sexually excited. She got me in my weak spot. We ended up kissing and making out. Damn. I felt good at that moment, but I felt bad on the inside. It had been over a year since I'd had sex. I can't believe I slept with a woman again. It's been a minute since I had sex with a woman. I got dressed and left right after we finished.

I told my friend what happened between me and Val. I never thought she was a lesbian. I thought she was really trying to be a friend to me. My friend was saying some rude things to me like she was jealous. She was the wrong person for me to tell what happened, when I used to sleep with her in the past. She was my first lesbian experience when I was younger. We used to sleep together from time to time. Sometimes I slept with her for pleasure, and sometimes I slept with her because I felt bad for her when she would call me crying. She had bad experiences with the men, from the stories she would tell me. I don't know why I would feel bad for her when she treats me like crap sometimes. But she was a childhood friend I grew up with. I tried to be there for her, no matter what.

Since Val and I slept together that one time, she had been calling me every day. She'd been popping up once in a blue with flowers for me on my bus route and then she would leave. We started hanging out more and having more sex with one another. It seemed like since I was messing with her, more women were hitting on me. I turned them down instantly because I didn't really want to live that lifestyle, not that anything was wrong with it. I just love men.

One day I went to see Val. When we had sex, she used a strap-on. I asked her why we had to use that. She said she wanted to please me.

"I don't want you to use a strap-on. You're not a man," I responded.

But she insisted and used it. I did not give her the response she was hoping for. I just laid there, upset. So we argued about the situation. I just ran and took a shower. As soon as I got a shower, she was right there to dry me off. Then she grabbed me by the hand and walked me back into her room. She rubbed me down with lotion, complimenting my body. I know she was just trying to make me feel good. I was big compared to her. Looking at her body, she looked good. She had a beautiful body. Her body was nice and tight, firm everything. She didn't have children. If she did, her body would probably look like mine, maybe.

Some days, I spent the night with her. I would check and see if my brother was going to be home. If he stayed home, I would stay, but if he had to go out, I went back home.

It scared me the way I was starting to catch feelings for this woman. She treated me better than a man, in my opinion. It was messing me up emotionally. I didn't want to be with a woman. I didn't want my children seeing me have relations with a woman. I was afraid my habit would rub off on them. She was making plans for us to be in a relationship, but I had to keep reminding her that I'm married. That we agreed to fun and pleasure only. Besides, I do not like going downtown on a woman. I do not like a woman's scent on my lips. I would cheat every time I had to go down on her—use more vibrator, less tongue. It worked every time; she would have a fast orgasm and push me off. I would run to the bathroom, brush my teeth, and wash my face. I did not want any scent of a woman on my face.

I cried almost every day. I wished my hubby treated me like this woman did. It had been a couple of months since she and I had been seeing each other. So I decided to invite her to my twins' birthday party. I also invited two of my coworkers who I became friends with and their children, and my favorite cousin and her child. Then I invited my childhood friend. Everyone showed up, even my childhood friend with two other females who were in the lifestyle. We were all having a good time, music playing, children having fun.

All of us adults were having a great conversation, all until my childhood friend said something fresh to me. I ignored her, but Val went off. She had the nerve to ask me why I was messing with that old lady when I could get with her. My friend Val was so upset. I had to make my childhood friend and her company leave. Then Val was ready to go. I told her I would take her home after all the guests leave. She just sat there in the chair all day, upset and with a mean expression on her face.

My two coworkers knew about my situation with her. One of them was lowkey trying to hit on me. Every time I went to her house she would be fresh talking and getting naked around me. I just ignored her.

But back to this party. My friend Val was 50 years old and I was 31 years old. Val did not look her age. She kept her hair done and worked out. I was glad that all the guests left except my cousin. She stayed at my house while I was taking Val home. Val started accusing me of cheating on her.

"How am I cheating on you when we are not even in a relationship? You do realize that I am married." I pulled out a cigarette and started smoking.

She was starting to stress me out. She was going off on me. I was not in the mood to argue.

Next thing I know, Val pulled out a ring and proposed to me.

"Are you trying to be funny? Are you really serious? I told you too many times, I am married. I am not leaving my husband for no woman. I love dick too much, sorry."

She started acting crazy. "Let me out the car."

"Okay, as soon as I get off the highway, I will let you out."

This crazy woman opened my car door while I was on the highway. I had to grab her.

"Are you fucking crazy? I am so done with you when I get off this highway. Don't call me anymore, don't get on my bus, don't come around me, period. Something is really wrong with you."

"I can't help the way I feel about you. I love you," Val responded.

I said, "I care for you too, but I don't want to live my life as a lie. I can't see me being with a woman, I just can't."

As soon as we got off the highway, I stopped the car. "You can get out now!"

"No, take me home," she screamed at me.

I took her home and went back to my house. I had to tell my cousin what happened.

"You need to leave that woman alone. She ain't nothing but trouble."

So I started dating some guy to get over my mess I was in with Val. Every time Val called me, I didn't pick up the phone. I changed my bus line, so I would not see her anymore.

One night, I was coming in the garage from working a line. I saw Val sitting in the lounge area waiting for me. I walked past her as if I didn't know her. I did my paperwork and started walking to my car. She followed me with some roses and apologized.

"How did you know what time I got off?"

"Your coworker told me."

"Wow, I thought we agreed to leave each other alone."

"Give me a ride home," she asked me.

So I let her in my car because I don't need anyone else in my business. While I was driving her home, she said, "Let's go to the bar and get a drink."

We ended up at the female Go-Go bar. I had two drinks and she had one. She paid for me to get a lap dance, and I sat there having fun. When it was time to leave, I let her drive my car, since I'd had four or five drinks and she only had one.

She drove us to her house and said, "You are spending the night because you've been drinking." She cut my car off and took my keys before I could respond. She went inside her house.

"Give me my keys," I asked her.

She said, "No, not until tomorrow."

I didn't know where she hid my keys. Next thing I know, she got undressed, and she undressed me. We both ended up having sex. How it ended, I don't know.

It was the next morning, and I had to go pick up my children from my cousin's house. My brother had to work a double.

*****

My husband will be home soon. I am excited. One more week to go. I told Val she has to leave me alone. "My husband will be home, and I can't see you no more." She was upset. She was threatening to tell my husband about me and her.

"Why would you do some shit like that? I told you everything."

Then she said she was going to come to my house and fuck shit up.

"If you come to my house, Val, me and you are going to really have a problem." I changed my phone number so she couldn't call me anymore.

I wanted to have the house looking nice before my hubby got home. I bought all my children a bedroom set. I was renting my bedroom set. I had some guy come over to paint the house only on the days my brother was home. I bought a new living room set and a small stereo system.

I got excited. I had to go pick my hubby up from the airport. As soon as we got home, I cooked dinner for the house. We had a good day; we even had sex that night. Finally got to have sex with my hubby.

Next thing I know, my phone was ringing back to back. I didn't answer. I saw that it was Val. I don't know how she got my new phone number. Later the next morning, I checked my voice mail. "I will be at your house to tell your husband everything." I got nervous and upset.

"Rudopho, I have to talk to you. While you were gone, I was seeing someone." He stopped what he was doing and sat next to me. I explained the whole story to him. Right when I was finished talking, the phone rang.

My husband picked up the phone. "Leave my wife alone, her husband is home."

I cried and explained why I did what I did. "I didn't mean to step outside of our marriage, I am sorry."

We sat there and prayed about the situation, and he forgave me. I was up under him, but our sex life was really changed.

*****

My vacation time is here. We are going to Atlanta to see his mother. I was excited to get out of New Jersey, for me and my children. I packed our bags the night before. I fried chicken and made fruit bags with oranges and grapes. I bought snacks, plenty of water, juices, and soda. Then we went to pick up a rental van.

We got on the road at 10:00 am. While driving, Rudopho started talking crazy and driving crazy, right when I almost fell asleep.

"What's wrong with you?" I asked.

"I can't believe that you had an affair."

"I'm sorry. I didn't mean for it to happen."

He kept going on and on about what I did.

"You know what? I don't want to go with you to Atlanta. Just drop me off at the nearest exit. I will go back home, me and my kids."

Thank God my children were asleep and did not hear any of this stuff. We pulled over to the next rest area in New Jersey, and I was waking my children up to go to the bathroom. I was going to call a taxi to pick up me and my children. He got out and walked around to my side of the car. Then he hugged me and apologized.

"Don't leave. I want you to go with me to Atlanta."

"I am driving all the way to Atlanta," I said.

After we used the bathroom, I got behind the wheel. I drove us all the way. I was tired; I'd only had six hours of sleep the night before. Every rest stop we went to, I bought myself two cans of energy drink. I was feeling energized.

As soon as we got to the south of the border, we got out to use the restroom and got something to eat. We took a lot of pictures, then we got back in the car. I kept driving. It was 6:00 am when we finally made it to Atlanta. I then pulled over at a store and said, "You can drive the rest of the way." We were now only 15 minutes away from his mom's house. I was tired now.

As soon as we pulled into the driveway, his mom greeted us at the door and gave us all a hug. Then we started unloading the car, and then me and my hubby took a nap. She entertained the kids, my children, and his daughter. When we got up, we all went sight-seeing, went out to eat, and got some ice cream, and went back to her house. Her husband was not there; he was out at work. We had a nice time out there in Atlanta. We went somewhere different every day.

When the end of the week came, we packed up to leave. While everyone got in the car, I ran back in and left $600.00 on her counter for her letting us stay with her. Then after all the hugs goodbye, we drove off.

She called us right back. She said, "Come back, you left your son's medicine."

I didn't want to go back, because I didn't want my hubby to know I left that money to her.

She said to me as she was bringing out the medicine, "I am going to get you."

"What did I do?" I responded.

"You left all that money on the counter. Why did you leave me that money?" she said.

"Because we used your water, lights, and we stayed at your place."

She said, "Take this money back."

"No, you keep it," I said.

She said, "No, it's too much."

I said, "It's okay."

She then said, "Well, take some of it back." Then she gave me back $300.00, and we drove off.

I wanted to stop and see my sister for one day before we went back to New Jersey. My sister was expecting us. She paid for my hotel. I didn't really want to stay at a hotel. I wanted to spend as much time as possible with my sister; I only got to see her once, sometimes twice a year since she moved to Virginia.

I drove us to Virginia and met my sister at the hotel. We had two hotel rooms attached, so my kids could just walk into our room. The room was $400.00. So, after my sister sat with us for about an hour, as she was leaving, I gave her the cashback that she'd spent on our rooms. The next day, we checked out of the hotel and went to spend the day with my sister. We had breakfast and an early dinner at her house. Once 5:00 pm came, we got back on the road. I wanted to spend the last four days at home relaxing from my two weeks' vacation.

As soon as we got home, we unloaded the car. I got my kids to bed, then I went to bed. The next morning, I received a phone call from my mother.

"What's wrong, Ma?"

She said she was about to get evicted from her apartment.

"Why?"

She responded that she did not pay her rent for about eight months.

I was upset with her. "Why, Ma?"

"None of your business, but can you help me?" she said.

"How much do you need?"

"$3,000, I need."

"Wow, that's a lot of money. I will call you back," I said.

"Hurry, or they going to lock me out tomorrow."

I called my sisters and brother to see how much they could spare. I didn't want to use the rest of my money for her rent. I only had $3,800.00 left. I saved up my money for a couple of months. I didn't know how much I was going to need for Atlanta and my children's school clothes. So far, after calling my siblings, they were not able to spare much. I only received $500.00 from them. I had to pay the rest because I did not want my mom to stay with me. I was very upset about my mother's situation. I had to pay $2,500.00 toward my mother's rent. My mother had the nerve to say she would pay me back.

"Please tell me how, Ma." She was still getting high.

After paying that lump sum, I didn't want my mother to go behind in her rent again. Every month I went and paid her rent with the money I worked for. I did it for six months straight. I didn't tell my husband. I didn't want him to be upset. We were already struggling with our bills.

Then I told my sister and cousin what I was doing to see if they could help out. My sister said, "Stop paying Mommy's rent. You are enabling her to keep getting high." She said, "Go to Mommy's house when she gets her check and make her pay her rent." So I went and had a talk with my mother, and told her she has to start paying her rent. She said okay and gave me her debit card.

I wished I never had this responsibility of having to help my mother out. Every time her check came on her debit card, she would call me at midnight to go pull her money out and bring it to her. I would be very tired, being I got off of work at 1:00 am. My schedule changed at work again.

We change our schedule every four months. I was glad to get off the bus route to New York. I had this one passenger, Albert, who was harassing me. He always got on my bus on the last trip to NY. Now, he was not harassing me in a bad way; he would just say, "Let me be your man." I always reminded him I'm married. He paid his fare and had a seat; we used to have a good conversation, nothing sexual. He would hang out with me for the round trip and get back off my bus and get on his nice motorcycle.

But this one day, Albert got on my bus, another passenger Jay happened to get on my bus who was also a regular. Me and Albert were having a regular conversation until Jay got on and joined in the conversation.

Albert asked me, "Who is this man being rude?"

I said, "A passenger, just like you are."

Albert had to say, "No, I'm your man."

I laughed and said, "You do know I am married."

When we got to the last stop in NY, Albert had the nerve to squeeze my ass and kiss me. He said I was his girl. I slapped him so hard in the face. He was trying to make my other passenger jealous when I was not trying to get with none of them. I just enjoyed the company on the bus with different passengers. Sometimes it was boring just riding the bus up and down with no one to chat with. Albert was so upset that he just walked away. I am not going to lie: he was so fine; he had long dreads down his back, complexion was very light-skinned, he had a muscular toned body, and was a little shorter than me. He was from the islands. But I was not feeling him like that. He had a nasty attitude.

After work, I would go to the ATM, then go take the cash to my mother, go home, and go to bed. Then the next day, I'd go back to her community, pay her rent, and go to the store and get her $100.00 worth of groceries. Then I would give her the rest of her money. In between going to visit my mother with my children, she had all these different people coming in my face, threatening me in front of my kids.

One said, "Your mother said you got my money," with a strap on his side.

I had to tell him how I do the money—pay her rent, buy her groceries—and then she gets the rest of the money. I also had to say, "Don't threaten me anymore, that's between you and my mother."

After dealing with the threatening phone calls and people coming in my face for six months, I went to my mother and gave her the debit card back. "Ma, you're on your own. Don't call me no more when you get behind in your rent."

She cussed me out, and I walked away. I was done. "I don't know these people. What kind of mother and grandmother are you, that you put me and my babies' lives in danger?"

*****

Back to my home situation, I came home from work and went straight to the kitchen, and my husband had the nerve to ask me what's for dinner.

"What? I need to be asking you this: you been home since 2:00 pm. Here it is 11:00 pm, I just got home."

"Well, I am hungry. Can you fix me something to eat?"

I was so angry. I grabbed two chicken legs out of the freezer, still in my uniform. I grabbed the knife to break it apart, then I threw the knife in the sink. My hubby jumped out of the way, thinking I was going to throw it at him. "Next time, cook your own self something to eat."

It was late. I cooked boiled chicken legs, rice, and string beans, and slammed his plate on the table. I went upstairs to go to bed. I was very tired and stressed out from arguing with my son's father. My son's dad called my son's cellular phone I bought him. I was driving my children home from the store from getting snacks before I went to work. While he was on the phone with his dad, he asked me to come to the phone.

"Tell him I am driving."

He asked me to come to the phone again.

"I am driving, Divin, tell your dad." My son Divin put the phone on speaker.

As soon as I said "what," he said, "You stupid bitch, all I want to know is what time today you going to bring my fucking son over."

"The court order says you can't get him until next week," I said.

He said, "Fuck that, you dumb bitch, I want my son today."

"No, you trifling-ass motherfucker, you get your son on the day the court ordered."

My son started crying out loud. I wish I could have a normal family like everyone else. I felt so bad, me and his dad could never have a normal conversation. We always argued every time we spoke to one another. He thinks he still can control me and tell me how to run my house or how to spend my money. But his ass doesn't pay his child support like he's supposed to. If he is not verbally abusing me, he's verbally abusing my son. I am so tired of him and his threats. On the days I drop him off to his dad's house on the court-ordered days, he never brings my son back home on time, or he argues with me to come to get my son because he is not bringing him home. Or when I do go pick my son back up, he's not at home. Why does he act like this?

I used to let him just pick my son up whenever my son wanted to go. All up until he just popped up at my house to pick my son up. I had to say no because I was taking my children to a birthday party, so he could not go. After arguing with me, he walked down the stairs and busted my window out of my car with his fist. I was so upset, I wanted to call the police on that stupid bastard. But I just let it go and got the window fixed, and went to his office with the receipt and he refunded me my money back. This asshole does not want to start a war with me.

I did not have to worry about my other children's dads. One was deported and the other pops up once a year, then he disappears again. I never knew how he would find out where I moved to. Rudopho just ignored us and never said anything about the situation with me and his dad; he stayed neutral.

Four months passed and I got a different shift, which gets me off work at 10:30 pm. I was under a lot of pressure from work. I was trying my hardest to keep my job, and trying to make this marriage work. Now I had more things to do throughout the day since my daughter is working. My son only worked on the weekends he went to his dad's house. I kept telling my son not to work for his dad.

Every time he worked for his dad, when it came time for him to pay my son, he would say, "Go ask your mother. I paid it on child support, so she has your money."

His dad pissed me off because now my son thinks the child support money is his pocket money he worked for. Me and his dad argued every time the child support payments came through once every three months. He only paid it after my son worked for him. My son was only 12 years old. He always asked me to drop the child support. Why would I drop the child support? He must be bugging. I paid more than his cheesy $78.00 he was supposed to pay once a week. I bought new clothes for my children, paid their medical bills, bought food, and gave them an allowance for keeping the house clean.

His other way of trying to get me to drop the child support was taking me to court every month faithfully. I asked the judge to please stop him from bringing me to court monthly; the judge replied he can do it as often as he wants. But it was causing me to miss days from work. It was too much. Between all this stuff I had to deal with and taking my daughter to work, and my son to his dad's house every other weekend, it was a lot.

I sit here and think about how did I get the time to do all of this? I thank God for his energy and strength. I felt like I was in it all by myself sometimes, that my son's dad just wanted to make my life miserable.

*****

I had to get a split schedule on the new bus pick. I picked a line that was on my children's route. My daughter who was in high school now had to walk her siblings to school and hurry and get to the bus stop. I bought my daughter a 2-zone bus card and my babies 2-zone student tickets. My children knew to get on my bus and have a seat close to me or sit in the long row next to each other. When my children got on my bus, it was normally my last trip on that line. After I finished my line out, I gave my oldest boy my car keys and told them to wait in the car. I ran in my garage and dropped off my paperwork and clocked out.

My daughter was at the age where she wanted to hang out and date. I would say to her, "Your books are your boyfriend and your education is your date. Enjoy." She was always upset with me, but I was afraid she would end up like me. One person said my daughter was going to end up like me, with a whole bunch of kids. That shit pissed me off. I don't want my children to struggle. Life was very hard for me. So I had to keep it real on the regular to my kids. I kept it real about sexually transmitted diseases.

My daughter did not like me too much. She and I used to clash from time to time. When she got paid, I had her give me $35.00 out of her check. Also on her paydays, I said, "Get what you need only, and bank the rest." Boy, did I make her upset. I didn't mean to. I wanted her and all my children to learn to save.

I taught my children from childhood to always speak their minds, and never bite their tongue for anyone, but do it in a respectful manner. Even when they talk to me, I allowed my children to voice their opinion. I wasn't taught that coming up. I always got popped in the mouth and was told to shut up. But my oldest daughter would say to me every chance she got, "I can't wait until I graduate to move out," because I did not let her run the streets. I didn't mean to be hard on her, but she was too young to go through the stuff I went through, and it still hurts me to this day, what I went through.

*****

Everything had gotten worse with the new situation I was in. I had to keep it to myself, but it was hurting me so bad. I had a couple of incidents/accidents at work. With the point system, I was holding onto my job by a thread. I had to do whatever I could do to keep my job. My marriage was on the rocks, and I was trying to find an apartment for me and my children without him.

But back to my job situation. I had an accident where I knocked on the mirror of the bus on two occasions. Some of the points were removed sooner. Since I had cried about my marriage situation to my boss, he worked it out where he and I started having a sexual affair. I needed my job, so I had to do what I had to do. I kept it quiet and did not say anything to anyone. A little suck here and there. His dick was so little and he came so fast, I was doing what I had to do. Most days, he just wanted to eat my kitty, my funky kitty. I'd be out there working all day and pissing in my cups because some of the lines don't have access to a bathroom, so you know my butt was funky.

After sleeping with him for a couple of years into working for the company, I guess he told his friend, who was another supervisor. I cussed his ass out and said, "I don't know what you are talking about." He would just pop up on me and say fresh remarks about how big my ass was, and he'd like to get a piece. I ended up sleeping with another supervisor, but not that nasty jerk that popped up on me. Then it went from sleeping with supervisors to sleeping with coworkers. I was now sleeping with four coworkers and two supervisors. I did not mean for this shit to happen at my job. How the fuck did I end up in this situation? I was getting so tired of the situation. More men were trying to get in on the action, but all I was trying to do was save my job.

Then after sleeping with one supervisor, I ended up catching feelings for him and the one coworker. Because if I needed anything, they gave it to me. I had to go to the emergency room one time and Rudopho would not take me. I couldn't hardly move, or put my panties on. So I called my coworker and he caught the cab to my house and drove my van to the hospital. He made me wait while he got me a wheelchair. He wheeled me inside the hospital and put my gown on. He did not care how I looked; my hair was matted and nappy, and I had snot and tears all over my face. He just cleaned my face and put a cap on my head. Another time he caught the cab to me was after I got my four wisdom teeth removed. Rudopho dropped me off and would not come pick me up. I was not allowed to leave unless someone got me, due to the anesthesia. I called my coworker, who was now my friend. Once again, he took a cab and got me. He took me to pick up my prescription, and the same cab brought us to my home. He stayed in the cab and then he went home after I got out. He was a very sweet guy. I hated that he was catching feelings for me.

The one supervisor that I was catching feelings for was getting reckless. He was popping up on my different routes with his son, and popping up around the corner from my house. He was even calling me all hours of the day. But if I needed something, he got it for me.

It was getting out of control, where one day I was sleeping with over four men in one day. I had to keep my purse stocked up with condoms of different sizes and brands. These nasty men didn't give a crap about me; all they cared for was when they were getting some ass. Most of the men were giving me money, but only two of the men gave me big money, $500 or better. I was not so bright and didn't know my rights. I had to keep sleeping with these now seven different men from my job. It got so bad, I started sleeping with random men for money who was on my bus. One of my supervisors knew when my break was and asked for sex. I hated that he felt he was entitled to get sex whenever he wanted it. But I needed my job, and I wanted to keep the peace with my job. I was also trying to make sure I had money to support my children.

People started talking about me at work; you know when women are talking about you. They'd be watching my every move in the garage. I am not proud of what I was doing. I was getting very tired of the situation. I was often depressed.

On my days off, after spending time with my children, after they went to bed I would sit in the living room and listen to my depressing music. I'd have a glass of wine or something stronger and sit and cry. I was so disgusted with my life and the situation at work and couldn't talk to anyone. I didn't know what to do and how to get out of the mess that I was in. I would often talk to God in my mind. I didn't know what I did that was so wrong. I wished I could do everything all over. I wished I did not use my body up so badly. I thank God that he kept me, even in my mess. I was very stressed and feeling very low about myself.

I didn't know why all these men wanted to sleep with me, and my own hubby didn't want to sleep with me. I felt horrible that I was married and I spread my body around like peanut butter spread on bread. I wished I was pretty, I wished I was skinny, I wished my hubby was attracted to me. He and I would have conversations and he would reassure me that he loved me. He would say it was all in my head, that I was stressing for nothing. I would convince myself to believe him, but his actions showed me otherwise. I even suggested that me and my hubby could have a threesome because he didn't like to sleep with me, but I couldn't understand why he wanted to be with me.

Love is not supposed to hurt. I knew he was sleeping around, but he just wouldn't tell me. He used to carry his phone everywhere he went, but he would run and answer my phone. I would give him evidence that I would find, and he was going out a lot since the beginning of our marriage.

I threw my cards on the table and told him I had an affair a couple of times. He stopped me and didn't want to hear anymore. He would just say, "Let's pray about it." We did pray about it. I was being honest because it was hurting me that I was stepping outside of my marriage.

I had done it for many reasons: one because my hubby would not touch me; two, I needed to make money because the bills were more than what I could afford; and three, it was the only way I could keep my job.

I was so sick and disgusted with myself. I couldn't stand to look at myself in the mirror. But now, I don't blame my husband for not wanting to sleep with me. Thank God he was the only man that stuck around. He toughed it out with me. He stayed even though the baby daddies left. He helped out with whatever he could help out with. Our relationship is so weird; I'm inside of my relationship and I don't understand it. It got to the point if a man would call me, he would answer the phone, say their name, and give the phone to me, or sometimes I would tell him to tell them I would call them back. He didn't say anything about the different men calling me. It was like he didn't even care, besides some of those men were my extra income.

My children didn't want for anything. I took them on trips, amusement parks, bought them the newest games and clothes, gave them birthday parties. Whatever they wanted, I tried my best to get it. I wanted them to have more than I ever had.

I was getting so sick of myself. I was getting very depressed. I even fucked up some of these men's hard-ons when I used to cry while they were fucking me. I would be fine when we got started. Next thing I know, my emotions took control. One guy who was my regular knew to have my alcohol ready before we got it in. He would play the music I liked so I'd be nice and mellow.

I went to the employee counseling to vent out my problems. Everything was confidential, so I told him almost everything.

I hated if I got in a situation where I had to borrow money from one of my coworkers. My name was spread so badly in my garage. On my days I had to work, I would just grab my things needed and hurry out to my bus. This one particular day, getting on my bus, this man came on my bus. I was getting tired of this shit. I was tired of everything. I was straight-up reporting any new men who thought that they, too, were going to get some ass from me. Nope, I have too many men on my plate; no room for more. I am done. I was afraid to tell my hubby about my situation at work. I just have to figure a way out of this shit.

I can't afford to pay for my one child's private school, which was $795.00 a month and my bills at home, kids' school clothes, and a lot of other bills. The reason his bill was that high was the public school tried to make my one son go to special education. I did not want that for him, so I put him in a private school. That only lasted for five months, because the struggle got really real.

I was even paying the rental place for another living room set, bedroom sets, and a new, bigger stereo. Now I have to buy a new window for my car; some crackhead busted my window out of my car. I just got me a membership to the gym. Today was my first time going, and it will be my last. I parked my car in the parking lot next to the other cars. I had to call the police and they took a report. Whoever came in my car stole my bookbag, which carried over 500 CDs. They stole what was left of my cigarettes and my $4.00 in coins. I checked in my visor; they didn't touch my $50.00. I was upset. I was driving all around the area, looking for my bookbag. If I saw the person with it, I was going to snatch my shit out of his or her hands.

I am now almost six years at this company. We moved again. Now we live in N. Newark. This house we were renting was horrible. I financed a new car and after only having my car for two weeks, my car window got busted into two times. The first time, it was to steal my temporary tag. The second time, the man who was working on the house next door, his workers made a mistake and busted my window carrying plywood.

The other problem with living there was mice and roaches. Then the biggest problem was the mold spores that grew in my kitchen. My one daughter kept having asthma attacks and the other daughter was coughing badly. I told the doctor about our living situation. She said we had to move. We had only lived in the place for four months. This house looked nice on the outside but it was very horrible to live in. I made several complaints to the company about the conditions. The carpet stunk and was very dirty, and the walls were never painted. Every time we used the kitchen sink, it leaked in the basement. The basement was full of water; it covered the tops of our shoes. It smelled like dead animals down in the basement, which made the entire house smell.

The owner of the company came out and had me move everything from upstairs to downstairs. Once I did that, he took photos. His crew came in and ripped up the carpet and threw everything outside the bedroom windows. He took out the kitchen sink and threw it out of the kitchen window. They fixed the floors in two days. But they would never come back to fix our kitchen sink. One month passed by, still no sink. I got tired of washing my meats in the bathroom tub and then having to scrub my bathtub with bleach. So I kept complaining to the company, and they never fixed my sink.

I then hired an attorney. I gave the attorney the fee he asked for. When it came time to go to court, my attorney was very horrible. He did not represent me. This slick ass man who owned the real estate on North 13th Street was a slick man. The pictures he took on the day he had me move everything downstairs, made it look like we kept the house a mess, that bastard. I was so upset. I was trying to explain how and when he took the photo. But his slick attorney was not trying to hear me. My attorney did not do or say anything. I was very upset. I was in there fussing, trying to explain everything. But the case was closed with both of us walking away with nothing. I wanted my security deposit back. That slick ass man, ugh he disgusts me.

Then the city did not help me. Code enforcement didn't help me. They just came out and took pictures and that's all. So we had 30 days to move out of the house. I called my dad and explained the whole situation to him. I started looking for a new place to move to.

Then Daddy's suggestion was why don't I move down to Ohio? I could look for somewhere close, and he could help me with my children until I got on my feet.

Then I also kept in mind, my grandma said to move to Florida with her. And my Auntie in Georgia suggested Georgia would be a great place to raise my children.

Where will we move, and how will I get up the money for the move? We started looking online and going to look in different towns. We even took weekend trips. Yes, I found it! The place I will move to. I was so excited for me and my family.

I was packing things in trash bags. We were throwing lots of stuff away. I had to throw out and give away almost everything. I gave away the computer, washer and dryer, living room set, and kitchen set. I gave away my favorite stereo. I washed all the clothes. I put everything in the small moving truck. I did not want to bring roaches or mice to my new location. We didn't take any furniture, just all our clothes.

I am excited about this new ride to our new home out of the State of New Jersey.

www.ingramcontent.com/pod-product-compliance
Lightning Source LLC
Chambersburg PA
CBHW061153170626
46809CB00003B/1077